Publishing

Other books in the Careers for the Twenty-First Century series:

Aeronautics
Art
Biotechnology
Computer Technology
Education
Emergency Response
Engineering
Film
Finance
Law
Law Enforcement
Medicine
Military
Music
The News Media

Careers
for the
Twenty-First
Century

Publishing

by Yvonne Ventresca

LUCENT BOOKS

An imprint of Thomson Gale, a part of The Thomson Corporation

THOMSON

™

GALE

Detroit • New York • San Francisco • San Diego • New Haven, Conn.
Waterville, Maine • London • Munich

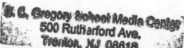

For more information, contact
Lucent Books
27500 Drake Rd.
Farmington Hills, MI 48331-3535
Or you can visit our Internet site at http://www.gale.com

LIBRARY OF CONGRESS CATALOGING-IN-PUBLICATION DATA

Ventresca, Yvonne.
  Publishing / by Yvonne Ventresca.
    p. cm. — (Careers for the twenty-first century)
  Includes bibliographical references and index.
  ISBN 1-59018-298-7 (alk. paper)
  1. Publishers and publishing—Vocational guidance—Juvenile literature. 2. Authorship—Vocational guidance—Juvenile literature. 3. Book industries and trade—Vocational guidance—Juvenile literature. I. Title. II. Series.
  Z278.V46 2005
  070.5'023—dc22

                                                                2004023421

Printed in the United States of America

Contents

Foreword

Young people in the twenty-first century are faced with a dizzying array of possibilities for careers as they become adults. However, the advances in technology and a world economy in which events in one nation increasingly affect events in other nations have made the job market extremely competitive. Young people entering the job market today must possess a combination of technological knowledge and an understanding of the cultural and socioeconomic factors that affect the working world. Don Tapscott, internationally known author and consultant on the effects of technology in business, government, and society, supports this idea, saying, "Yes, this country needs more technology graduates, as they fuel the digital economy. But . . . we have an equally strong need for those with a broader [humanities] background who can work in tandem with technical specialists, helping create and manage the [workplace] environment." To succeed in this job market young people today must enter it with a certain amount of specialized knowledge, preparation, and practical experience. In addition, they must possess the drive to update their job skills continually to match rapidly occurring technological, economic, and social changes.

Young people entering the twenty-first-century job market must carefully research and plan the education and training they will need to work in their chosen careers. High school graduates can no longer go straight into a job where they can hope to advance to positions of higher pay, better working conditions, and increased responsibility without first entering a training program, trade school, or college. For example, aircraft mechanics must attend schools that offer Federal Aviation Administration–accredited programs. These programs offer a broad-based curriculum that requires students to demonstrate an understanding of the basic principles of flight, aircraft function, and electronics. Students must also master computer technology used for diagnosing problems and show that they can apply what they learn toward routine maintenance and any number of needed repairs. With further education, an aircraft mechanic can gain increasingly specialized licenses that place him or her in the job market for positions of higher pay and greater responsibility.

In addition to technology skills, young people must understand how to communicate and work effectively with colleagues or clients from diverse backgrounds. James Billington, librarian of Congress, asserts that "we do not have a global village, but rather a globe on which there are a whole lot of new villages . . . each trying to get its own place in the world, and anybody who's going to deal with this world is going to have to relate better to more of it." For example, flight attendants are increasingly being expected to know one or more foreign languages in order for them to better serve the needs of international passengers. Electrical engineers collaborating with a sister company in Russia on a project must be aware of cultural differences that could affect communication between the project members and, ultimately, the success of the project.

The Lucent Books Careers for the Twenty-First Century series discusses how these ideas come into play in such competitive career fields as aeronautics, biotechnology, computer technology, engineering, education, law enforcement, and medicine. Each title in the series discusses from five to seven different careers available in the respective field. The series provides a comprehensive view of what it is like to work in a particular job and what it takes to succeed in it. Each chapter encompasses a career's most recent trends in education and training, job responsibilities, the work environment and conditions, special challenges, earnings, and opportunities for advancement. Primary and secondary source quotes enliven the text. Sidebars expand on issues related to each career, including topics such as gender issues in the workplace, personal stories that demonstrate exceptional on-the-job experiences, and the latest technology and its potential for use in a particular career. Every volume includes an "Organizations to Contact" list as well as annotated bibliographies. Books in this series provide readers with pertinent information for deciding on a career and as a launching point for further research.

Publishing: A Dynamic Industry

Publishing offers employment opportunities to a diverse population. Publishers are producing more books in the United States than ever before. An estimated 175,000 new books and revised editions were published in 2003, a 19 percent increase from the previous year. For each of those 175,000 books, there were writers, editors, agents, designers, and salespeople along the way who transformed an idea into a tangible book available to the public. Each person involved in publishing a book contributes different skills, but all have in common a love of books.

Diversity Among Publishing Careers

In general, the publishing industry generates a variety of materials, including magazines, newspapers, and directories. In addition to traditional print formats, the industry's expansion into electronic media has resulted in items such as audiobooks and Web-based news articles.

Book publishing encompasses a variety of book types. Trade publishing produces books for a general readership. Children's publishing ranges from picture books for young readers to edgy novels for older teens. Publishers produce reference books and textbooks for libraries and schools. Book publishing involves all of these areas and much more.

Careers in book publishing are as diverse as the books themselves. For each book produced, a writer labors over the words. An agent may be involved in finding just the right publisher for the writer's work. An editor helps perfect the manuscript and a designer crafts each visual element of the book. Salespeople negotiate with bookstores, libraries, and other buyers to enable the final package to reach its ultimate destination: the reader.

Changes in the Business

Determining what topics interest readers is an ongoing challenge. By 2008, annual consumer spending on books is expected to reach $44 billion. Still, sales of some types of books, such as adult hardcovers and mass market paperbacks, decreased slightly in 2003. "There's more and more competition for time,"[1] says Albert Greco, professor of media management at Fordham University in New York. He is referring to surveys that show, for example, more time spent on the Internet by the average American than time spent reading.

As readers' tastes have changed, so too has the publishing business. Consolidation has reduced the number of major New York–based publishing companies to a handful of giants. Technology

Small publishing companies such as Just Us Books, Inc. can offer opportunities to work with specialized publishers.

has affected the design, production, and selling of books. As the industry continues to evolve, the careers offered will also evolve.

Even as some areas within book publishing will experience slowed growth over the next several years, others, such as textbook publishing, can expect growth to accelerate. This is due to an increased number of high school and college students. Changes in what students are expected to learn will also create demand for new textbooks.

Although most of the professional jobs (as opposed to manufacturing and administrative jobs) in all kinds of publishing are expected to increase modestly through 2012, competition for book publishing jobs is high, since large numbers of college graduates possess the basic skills demanded. This is true despite the fact that pay at the entry level is often low. Judith Appelbaum, author of *How to Get Happily Published*, summarizes the appeal of a career in book publishing:

> A book, after all, is not just something that is. A book is something that does. Books show parents how to be better role models, hikers how to find the best trails, and politicians how to focus on tomorrow's problems instead of yesterday's. They spirit us away from everyday life to realms as diverse as Middlemarch and Middle Earth. They deliver information, insight, ideas, analyses, aesthetic experience, excitement, and more.
>
> If you think the world needs these things, then you'll probably enjoy being part of the production and delivery system. And those of us already working to connect writers with readers will be happy to have you on board.[2]

Chapter 1

The Writer: Creating Content

The written word is what book publishing is all about. Publishers rely on writers' words as the basis of their business. Images of writers scribbling notes at outdoor cafés, meeting with famous experts to gather research material, and signing autographs for fans conjure up the glamorous side of writing. While these events may occur, the reality is that writing is a disciplined process of capturing thoughts and research in a first draft, then revising and transforming that draft into a final manuscript. "Writing is not magic, but perseverance,"[3] says novelist Richard North Patterson. While a book may seem to flow effortlessly when it is read, that quality is the culmination of a great deal of hard work.

Where Do Writers Get Their Ideas?

That hard work begins as the writer hones the basic idea for a book, even before touching the computer keyboard. The most common question writers probably hear is, "Where do you get your ideas?" There is no single method for writers to create their stories. They can use any technique that works for them.

For Marcia Preston, who is a mystery novelist as well as the publisher and editor of *ByLine*, a magazine for writers, the writing process starts with the question, "What if?" For instance, "What if this crime happens, and it looks like an accident, or nobody can explain it, or nobody seems to care? What secrets did the victim have that might have caused this to happen?"[4]

A writer jots down thoughts in a notebook as he stares out at the ocean. Most writers carry a notebook with them at all times.

By asking these types of questions, a writer can brainstorm the story's plot.

Best-selling horror fiction writer Stephen King provides some "what if" examples from his own work. "*What if* vampires invade a small New England village? (*Salem's Lot*) . . . *What if* a young mother and her son become trapped in their stalled car by a rabid dog? (*Cujo*)"[5] Starting with the "what if" approach can help generate unique ideas.

An idea can sometimes start with the writer's vision of a character or characters. What do they look like, what motivates them, what quirks do they have? What makes them angry or disappointed? What prevents them from meeting their goals?

No single creative approach suits every writer. Many will roughly outline the plot before they begin; some create a detailed map of events; still others start writing and go where the story leads them.

Nonfiction Ideas

Even though nonfiction writers focus on factual material, the generation of ideas is still a creative process. Nonfiction writers can explore almost any subject that interests them, such as a sport, a period in history, or a specific person. Ideas can also come from the news or from talking to other people. Freelance writer Kelly Milner Halls recalls that when she interviewed a paleontologist for the *Chicago Tribune*, "He told me about Leonardo, the most complete dinosaur ever found, with 70 percent of his soft tissue fossilized along with his bones. A dinosaur mummy, I thought."[6] Her nonfiction book, *Dinosaur Mummies: Beyond Bare-Bone Fossils*, was the outcome of her research and her longtime interest in dinosaurs.

Initial Research

For both nonfiction and fiction, research follows the generation of basic ideas. Before nonfiction writers research an entire book, they

Horror writer Stephen King has generated engaging story ideas by building a plot around an imagined scenario.

do enough investigation to make sure they have a book-worthy topic. Most writers increase their chances of success when they choose a topic that genuinely interests them. They start by writing a proposal, which they then submit to publishers. A proposal typically includes a statement about the book's focus, a detailed outline, and information about experts and sources the writer plans to consult. The writer may even submit one or two sample chapters, depending on the publisher's requirements. In addition, nonfiction writers explore what books already exist on their chosen subject, so they can explain how their book will stand out from similar publications.

For about eighteen months Shaunda Kennedy Wenger and her coauthor Janet Kay Jensen researched the proposal for *The Book Lover's Cookbook*, which features recipes for dishes mentioned in literature. After searching for excerpts they could use, Wenger and Jensen contacted published writers and asked for recipes and anecdotes to accompany the text they wanted to quote. They were able to correspond with authors such as Richard Peck, who helped them adapt a recipe for the cherry tarts made by his character (from *A Year Down Yonder*) Grandma Dowdel. Since this was their first book, they felt their innovative approach and the participation of published authors would make the package appealing to a publisher. They continued this research process after their proposal was accepted.

Research Methods

Writers often research their topic by consulting experts. For example, when Halls worked on *Dinosaur Mummies*, she interviewed more than thirty paleontologists, museum staffers, and geology experts at universities.

Not surprisingly, writers do a great deal of research in libraries. To research her book *Turn of the Century*, Ellen Jackson investigated what life was like for children living at the turn of each century during the last millennium in Great Britain and the United States. With a librarian's guidance, she found a number of books on social history and customs that explained what daily life was like during different times. Jackson examined each century individually, figuring out where to find the facts she needed and determining which information to include. She learned, for example, that in 1600 there were no dentists. Barbers cut people's hair, and

Nonfiction writers do much of their research at the library, where they have access to a number of resources.

when necessary pulled teeth, too—a detail she was able to use in her book.

Writers sometimes face the problem of discovering conflicting information in their research. For example, Jackson spent time trying to find out how many ice cream flavors were available in the year 1900, a detail she needed for one story. Various sources disagreed with each other, so she narrowed her research to ice cream in Pennsylvania, her setting for that story, and found a consistent answer. (Flavors available in most places were vanilla, strawberry, chocolate, cherry, and a mixed fruit called tutti-frutti.)

Writers, especially those focusing on nonfiction, should be skilled at fact-finding, taking notes, and explaining difficult concepts. Organizing research materials is important for keeping facts and sources straight. Accuracy is essential, and nonfiction writers must check facts with multiple sources. During the research process, nonfiction writers may also be required to locate relevant images to accompany the text. For example, Halls would ask the experts she interviewed if they had photographs or knew where she could obtain them, and their information led to the pictures that were included in *Dinosaur Mummies*.

Research is also integral to the fiction-writing process. Correct facts are crucial for a story to be believable. For example, when award-winning author Deborah Hopkinson was preparing to write *The Klondike Kid* series, she read diaries and unpublished accounts of the Klondike gold rush from the University of Washington's library. "That helped me to see what it was like to be there,"[7] Hopkinson says, and it allowed her to add authentic details to her historical adventure.

The First Draft

After brainstorming, researching, and deciding the basic elements of the book,writers are ready to begin the first draft. For Anthony Tedesco, coauthor of *Online Markets for Writers: How and Where to Get Published Online and Paid for It*, writing "raw, streaming first drafts"[8] is his favorite part of the process. Imperfect writing is okay at this point, because the writer will revise it many times. "I don't worry too much about getting it down perfectly, because I know I'll be coming back later to the next drafts," says Robin Friedman, author of *How I Survived My Summer Vacation: And Lived to Write the Story*. "That is one reason so many writers freeze up when writing. They feel they need to be writing the actual novel immediately, when, in reality, it's just the first draft they have to do."[9]

The Revision Process

The first draft is only the beginning of the writing process. Writers review their work and modify it many times before submitting it to a publisher. Writers must objectively reread what they have written and question themselves: Is the dialogue realistic? Is the main character interesting? Is additional research necessary? They examine these types of details, and then they rewrite and review it again.

Many writers find it helpful to let someone else read the book and provide feedback. Some writers join critique groups in which members review each other's writing. Not only do they get advice, they also learn how to improve their writing from analyzing other people's work. Taking criticism is not easy, even when it is constructive. Hearing that a reader does not like or does not understand parts of a book can be difficult. Sometimes the criticism is contradictory; six members of a critique group can give six different opinions. The writer must evaluate what changes would benefit the story the most.

Based on critiques and on their own analyses, writers will revise their work multiple times. For example, Friedman rewrote *How I Survived My Summer Vacation* seven times. There is no standard

Writing is a long and involved process. Writers like this woman typically spend many hours at the computer revising their work.

number of revisions or a specified amount of time to take. Regardless of the writer's exact process, each book requires discipline and persistence to finish.

Learning Where to Submit

When the manuscript is complete, a first-time novelist or picture-book writer begins looking for a publisher. Unpublished writers face the problem of getting the attention of an editor.

To help get their work read, writers sometimes ask a literary agent to represent them. A respected agent will submit the manuscript (or proposal) to editors on behalf of the writer, often getting faster results. Although the Association of Authors' Representatives has hundreds of agents as members, finding an agent can be difficult for first-time writers. Due to the volume of manuscripts they receive, agents can be particular about whom they sign on as a client.

Because of the difficulty of getting an agent, many writers try to find a publisher themselves. This avenue somewhat limits the number of potential publishers, because while some publishers are open to receiving submissions directly from writers, others only accept projects through agents.

The process for finding an agent or a publisher is similar. Writers must research who would be interested in their work. They often refer to directories, such as *The Literary Market Place* or *The Novel & Short Story Writer's Market*, to aid them in their search. Writers also check industry magazines and Web sites for current information about publishers. They request and review publishers' catalogs to determine which types of books certain publishers have accepted in the recent past. By attending conferences when possible, writers also meet editors and learn about their current needs. Studying publishers and the market is an ongoing process.

Submissions

Once a writer has analyzed who would be most interested in the book, the next step is to put together a package based on what each editor (or agent) prefers. Some editors request a query letter. This letter briefly describes what the book is about and provides information about the writer's background. If an editor is interested, then he or she will request the complete manuscript.

Other editors may ask for the whole manuscript up front with a brief cover letter.

Nonfiction writers rarely submit an entire manuscript. Instead, they write and submit a detailed proposal that outlines the planned content of the book. Only after being offered a contract does the nonfiction writer produce a first draft.

Rejections

Whether a writer submits a fiction manuscript or a proposal for a work of nonfiction, rejections are inevitable. Because each writing project is unique, even authors who have been published before may have a manuscript rejected. After Friedman sold her first novel, for example, twenty-two editors turned down her picture book *The Silent Witness* before it was accepted.

Many authors who subsequently became famous had their initial work rejected numerous times. Theodor Geisel, better known by his pen name, Dr. Seuss, was on his way home to burn his first manuscript, which had received twenty-seven rejections. Fortunately for Geisel, he happened to meet an old classmate who worked as an editor. That editor's decision to give Geisel a chance led to the publication of what became *And to Think That I Saw It on Mulberry Street*. Even more famous books such as *Green Eggs and Ham* and *The Cat in the Hat* followed from Geisel.

Sometimes even a negative response can lead to something positive. For example, Sudipta Bardhan submitted a picture book manuscript to an editor who was interested in both fiction and nonfiction. The editor rejected the picture book, but noticed Bardhan's background in biology from her cover letter. She contacted Bardhan and asked if she would be willing to write a book on science fair experiments for kids. Bardhan's *Championship Science Fair Projects: 100 Sure-to-Win Experiments* was the result.

Getting Paid

Even when a writer gets a manuscript accepted, how much money the project earns for the author varies widely. Some writers enter a work-for-hire arrangement. This means the publisher pays the writer a flat fee to write the book. The author typically receives payment

Author Judy Blume Discusses Censorship

One problem that writers face is censorship. Librarians may respond to complaints about a book's content by removing it from the school or public library shelves. Complaints typically stem from a parent or religious organization who challenges whether or not the book should be available to young people. According to the American Library Association, the ten most frequently challenged authors in 2003 were Phyllis Reynolds Naylor, J.K. Rowling, Robert Cormier, Judy Blume, Katherine Paterson, John Steinbeck, Walter Dean Myers, Robie Harris, Stephen King, and Louise Rennison. As a frequently challenged author, Judy Blume offers the following thoughts on censorship (excerpted from Judy Blume's introduction to Places I Never Meant to Be: Original Stories by Censored Writers *).*

What I worry about most is the loss to young people. If no one speaks out for them, if they don't speak out for themselves, all they'll get for required reading will be the most bland books available. And instead of finding the information they need at the library, instead of finding the novels that illuminate life, they will find only those materials to which nobody could possibly object. In this age of censorship I mourn the loss of books that will never be written, I mourn the voices that will be silenced—writers' voices, teachers' voices, students' voices— and all because of fear.

when the publisher accepts the manuscript. The fee is the same regardless of how well or poorly the book sells.

The more common type of payment for a writer is royalties. Royalties are basically a percentage of the book's price. Several factors determine the royalty amount, including the type of book, whether or not the writer has been published before, the writer's reputation and previous sales history, and the publisher's estimation of how well the book will sell.

Usually the author receives some of the royalties even before the book is published. This cash payment is known as an advance, and it is paid in installments before the book's publication. An advance is like an interest-free loan, since the writer receives some of the royalty money up front. A writer does not make any additional money until the advance is earned back. This means the publisher pays the writer no other money until the book has sold enough copies to generate royalties that exceed the advance.

In general, for a first hardcover novel for children, for example, the advance is about $5,000. For a first picture book, writers may receive a $3,000 to $8,000 advance. Advances for adult fiction fall into a wide range. "So much of it depends upon the kind of fiction and the quality of the writing," says literary agent Elaine English. "Small presses often pay little or no advances, for example, but the sky's the limit with a truly great commercial novel with unlimited potential."[10]

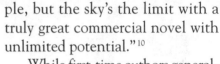

Best-selling novelist John Grisham now earns large sums of money for his work. Early in their careers, most authors earn very little.

While first-time authors generally receive small advances, subsequent books may bring larger ones. Best-selling author John Grisham received a $15,000 advance for his first book, *A Time to Kill*. His advance jumped to $600,000 for his second novel, *The Firm*. Grisham says of his good fortune, "I walked out of my law office without turning off the lights, and I have never looked back."[11]

Nonfiction advances also vary greatly depending on the type of publisher and the intended audience. The low end of nonfiction trade book advances is about $5,000.

Like advances, royalties across various genres can differ, with 10 percent being the most typical for hardcover books. Writers may be able to negotiate an increased royalty rate for higher sales (10 percent for the first five thousand copies of the book sold, 12.5 percent for the next five

thousand copies, and 15 percent after that, for example). If the project is a picture book, the writer splits the royalties with the illustrator, since the illustrations are a key part of the work. Depending on the quantity and source of photographs or illustrations in a nonfiction book, the nonfiction writer may be required to split the royalties as well.

A best-selling book can make the writer wealthy. For example, Harry Potter creator J.K. Rowling earned over $200 million in roy-

J.K. Rowling promotes her latest Harry Potter title at a bookstore in Scotland in 2003. Rowling's success has made her one of the world's wealthiest women.

Having the Confidence to Write

Anthony Tedesco is the coauthor of Online Markets for Writers: How and Where to Get Published Online and Paid for It *(Marketsfor Writers.com Press) and cofounder of the Student Publishing Program (225pm.org), a nationwide high school creative writing program. He offers the following advice for aspiring writers:*

Know that writing is more about confidence and perseverance than innate skills. You need the confidence to submit your work for consideration and the confidence to persevere through inevitable rejections and criticism. Read writing by your contemporaries to help recognize that you have what it takes now to be a writer. It's about connecting with people using words more than stringing together fancy, grammatically correct phrase-like-things. As long as people can understand what you're saying, say 'em however you want to. It's your voice we want to hear.

alties in 2003 and was declared richer than the Queen of England. This is not the case for the typical writer, however. "Don't quit your day job" is frequent advice to writers, meaning that they cannot expect to earn a living from their book writing alone. Hopkinson, who has had more than fifteen picture books published, points out that the 5 percent royalty a writer receives for each sixteen-dollar picture book sale is only eighty cents. She works full time to earn additional income and writes evenings and weekends, as do many other writers.

Book Promotion

Just how much a writer earns can be affected by the marketing efforts for a book. The publisher may have a publicist on staff to submit press releases and send out copies of the book to reviewers. For big-name authors like J.K. Rowling, publishers typically budget a great deal of money for publicity. Less well-known writers may have to do more of their own promotions.

To promote their books authors may visit bookstores, autographing copies of their book that customers have purchased. They may try to arrange television, radio, or newspaper interviews about their work. They may also write articles related to the book's topic. For example, to publicize their cookbook, Wenger and Jensen were able to write several articles about food, writing, and literature that a variety of magazines and newsletters published.

Writers can visit schools, libraries, and community centers to discuss their books and read excerpts. They may have props to help make the presentation more fun. For example, Hopkinson often brings items related to her books: a box of antique kitchen utensils (*Fannie in the Kitchen*), a bluebird box (*Bluebird Summer*) or a replica of Sweet Clara's quilt (*Sweet Clara and the Freedom Quilt*). Since these kinds of visits and presentations typically earn the writer a fee, they help writers gain extra income, sell their books, and become acquainted with their readers.

Traits of Successful Writers

Writers need certain traits to succeed. For example, because writers are self-employed, they must be disciplined enough to begin, revise, and complete a writing project. Friedman recommends that aspiring writers need patience to wait for editors and agents to respond, and should be able to handle rejection without taking it personally. She also notes that to make writing rich with real-life details, writers must be observant, and they must be persistent to achieve success.

Preparing for a Career as a Writer

Successful authors come from a variety of backgrounds, and not all receive formal training. Some read the numerous writing books available and work to apply what they have read to their own writing.

Other writers, however, do set out to study writing and achieve a related college degree. As many as two hundred colleges and universities across the United States offer undergraduate majors in creative writing. Numerous other schools offer degrees in English with a minor or concentration in writing.

Typical classes in a creative writing program include those that teach technical skills (such as the structure of the story line), literature courses, and writing workshops. In a workshop setting, students write an assignment and then present their work for discussion in class. Workshop subjects vary by the type of writing, such as poetry, fiction, playwriting, and nonfiction.

Those interested in writing nonfiction may choose to major in the area they are interested in (such as science or history) and take writing courses to supplement their learning of factual material. Journalism classes, such as newswriting and reporting, may also be suitable for nonfiction writers. Some creative writing programs offer a nonfiction concentration, so someone who is mostly interested in that genre might consider attending a school that provides that option.

Reading for Writing

Another key to preparing for this career is developing the habit of reading. An avid reader will "pick up a feeling for good writing, story structure, and love of language,"[12] says Marcia Preston. These skills are not necessarily taught in the classroom.

Some aspiring writers learn their craft in a university setting. Here, students in a creative writing class review and critique the work of their peers.

Sherry Garland explains in her book *Writing for Young Adults* how reading can benefit writers. Although she is advising writers who want to focus on a teenage or young adult (YA) audience, her suggestions about what to read and why apply to other writers as well. "Start with the Newbery winners [an award for excellence in children's literature] and the books that get the starred reviews (the stars beside a review signify excellence), but don't stop there," Garland says. She suggests,

---

Avoiding Writing Scams

Book publishing is a relatively unregulated field. Unethical individuals often try to take advantage of this to make money at the expense of unwary writers. The following excerpt is from Victoria Strauss's article, "Writer Beware." Strauss is a novelist and the creator of the Writer Beware Web site for the Science Fiction and Fantasy Writers of America.

When You Should Be Suspicious:
- If a literary agent requires an upfront fee.
- If a publisher offers a contract that requires you to bear all or part of the cost of publication. Authors who pay to publish are not taken seriously.
- If an agent or publisher recommends a service for which you have to pay.
- If you are asked to buy something as a condition of publication.
- If a book doctor or independent editor claims a manuscript must be professionally edited to have a chance with a publisher or agent.
- If you are solicited. Reputable agents, publishers and book doctors are overwhelmed with submissions, and have no reason to go out and look for more.
- If reasonable requests for information are refused.
- Remember the cardinal rule of writing. Money flows toward the writer. The only place you should ever sign a check is on the back!

The complete article is available at www.sff.net/people/Victoria Strauss/beware.html.

Read YA paperback series—mysteries, horrors and romances. Discover what characterizes each genre. This will help you find your niche. Read hardcover and paperback books. Read old classics and new best-sellers. Read books by the great YA authors of today and yesterday, and read the ones you've never heard of. If you find something you think is terrible, use it as an example of what not to do. If you read something inspiring and moving, use it as an example of what to strive for. . . . Read to learn how good authors handle dialogue, plot, pacing, and characterization. [13]

Getting Started

Even after years of reading and preparation, it can be difficult to become established as a novelist. One option for aspiring young writers is to form a group to discuss and encourage writing. They can learn their craft by studying books about technique. Most important, they can practice writing. Starting small is a good first step. Composing articles, conducting interviews for school newspapers, and creating stories and poems all help build communication skills. Keeping a private journal is another way to explore the craft.

In addition, many Web sites and magazines publish work by young writers. Entering contests can motivate writers to complete a project, and achieving publication can encourage writers to continue.

It often takes years of practice to write well. Friedman says, "You wouldn't expect training for the Olympics to be easy, right? It's the same with writing." [14] Excellence in writing, although hard to achieve, can provide a sense of satisfaction and fulfillment.

Chapter 2

The Literary Agent: Connecting Writers with Publishers

Literary agents serve as the bridge between writers and publishers. When agents successfully place a manuscript or book proposal, they provide an invaluable service to both sides. Having an agent enables a writer to spend time creating instead of researching publishers and marketing the manuscript to various editors. Meanwhile, the editor, who is inundated with submissions, trusts that the agent will only send material that meets the editor's requirements. "In a nutshell, an agent's job is to sell an author's work to the best publisher possible on the best terms possible," says literary agent Deborah Grosvenor of the Grosvenor Literary Agency, "and then do whatever he or she can through publication and beyond to ensure that the book reaches its broadest market."[15]

Evaluating Manuscripts

Agents must be choosy about whom they represent. Like editors, agents look for outstanding work among the large quantity of manuscripts they receive. Because they earn income only from the manuscripts they successfully place with publishers, agents must be able to recognize a manuscript or proposal that will sell.

Experienced agents say that screening manuscripts is more of an art than a science. Betsy Lerner, who works for an agency called the Gernert Company, says that an agent can respond to a number of manuscript qualities: the way it is written, the originality of the story, and the book's marketability, for example.

For Barry Goldblatt, who founded the Barry Goldblatt Literary Agency, evaluating manuscripts leads to both the best and worst parts of the job. "The best part," he says, "is finding new authors and bringing books . . . to life. Finding those gems and making sure readers out there get to read them. That's what it's all about." The worst part for him is reading unsolicited submissions, or what agents and editors call slush. "There's no question about it," Goldblatt says. "[Reading slush] is the part I would happily give up, if I could. But you can't. You never know, there might be a gem in there, you have to keep doing it."[16]

Hillary Clinton signs copies of her autobiography in 2003. Clinton's literary agent arranged this book signing to help boost sales.

Offering Editorial Advice

After taking on a writer as a client, an agent may request changes to make the work stronger and more marketable before trying to present the completed manuscript (for a fiction book) or proposal (for a nonfiction book) to a publisher. Erin Murphy, who founded the Erin Murphy Literary Agency, feels she increases her clients' chances of success if she refines their work before sending it to editors.

Agents, then, have some editorial functions, due to the competitive nature of the industry. An edited manuscript stands a better chance of acceptance than a less polished version. Agents also edit because of the time constraints editors face. "Agents are doing the work formerly done by editors, who are under increasing pressure to acquire [sign up new authors], rather than edit,"[17] says Grosvenor.

A literary agent discusses her client's writing over dinner. Literary agents sometimes suggest editorial changes to an author's manuscript before it is submitted to publishers.

Matchmaking

After the writer and the agent have agreed upon the necessary changes, the writer completes the revisions and the agent moves into his or her next role: matchmaker. One of the primary services an agent provides a writer is finding a publisher to buy the book. This is the point where the agent's work starts to pay off in a concrete way: Only when a publisher offers the writer a contract and pays an advance does the agent earn any money.

To play matchmaker effectively, agents must be aware of editors' specific tastes and current needs. Goldblatt says, "Part of what I bring to the table is a knowledge of these editors, who they are, what they like, what kinds of books they published in the past, and so who is the most likely to be interested in what my client has written."[18] Within each publishing house an editor may have a niche or an expertise with certain types of books. Agents' familiarity with various editors helps them target their submission efforts.

Keeping Up with Editors' Needs

Part of the agent's job is keeping track of changes in the publishing industry. Agents must be aware of mergers between publishing companies, downsizing, and personnel changes among editors. They can do this by reading industry publications, for example, and through personal networking. "You subscribe to all the magazines, you stay online, you do a lot of [meetings over] lunches," says Goldblatt. "You've got to keep your finger on the pulse."[19]

Not only must agents keep up with the publishing business, they must also be up-to-date on what people are reading. Murphy, who specializes in children's books, keeps up with editors and market trends in a variety of ways. "I communicate with many editors via email. I keep in touch with some booksellers, librarians, and teachers to hear what they wish they had to sell," she says.

> I'm on several list-servs online, where I communicate with others about what they are reading and loving. I watch TV shows that kids love to watch, keep an eye on the commercials, and so forth, so I can anticipate what kids might want in the next couple of years. In other words, I do the same things editors do, so I'm anticipating in the same way they

Author of children's books Angela Seward relies on her literary agent to keep her up-to-date on changing trends within the children's literature genre.

are. And then I talk by phone or email with editors about what they are working on, what they wish they had, and see their books when I meet with them through the year. [20]

Negotiating Contracts

The agent's ultimate goal is to place a promising manuscript with the right editor. Still, that is not the end of the agent's job. As an author's representative, the agent negotiates the publishing contract for the writer. "Remember publishing contracts are drafted by publishers and, therefore, typically protect the publisher best," says Elaine English, managing partner of the Graybill & English agency. "It is the agent's job to get the best deal possible for her author." [21]

The agent will initially settle details such as the advance, royalty rates, delivery dates, and payment schedule. The agent and the editor will also discuss what additional rights the publisher will buy (such as subsequent paperback rights) and what percentages the writer will earn on them.

After the agent negotiates these significant items, the publisher sends the agent a copy of the contract to review. If the agent has worked with the publisher before (on the behalf of previous clients, for example), than the agent will be familiar with the contract and may have already negotiated a standard version of it, called a boilerplate. In this case the agent reviews the existing base contract and checks the major items that the agent and the publisher have discussed. If it is the first time an agent has dealt with a publisher, then the agent spends time working with someone in the contracts department to refine the standard contract.

Throughout the contract negotiation the agent serves as the go-between for the writer and the publisher. When the contract is

Diversity in Publishing

Ethnic diversity among agents is vital, since some people feel there is a lack of diversity in the publishing industry. Janell Walden Agyeman, an African American literary agent with Marie Brown Associates, says in an interview with the author,

Agents play a crucial role in the publishing industry because we participate in the "gatekeeper" role assumed by the editors who acquire projects for the publishers. Because we help to identify projects we think worthy of publication, our tastes and interests directly impact the quality and scope of projects that eventually get published via "conventional" general trade publishers. . . .

When compared to the demographic composition of America, the proportions of the most visible ethnic and racial minorities in the book publishing arena continue to lag behind their numbers in the general population. . . . There continues to be a need for and room for individuals of all American racial and ethnic minorities to be involved in the book publishing industry.

finalized, the agent sends it to the writer to review and sign. The agent's services do not end, however, once the contract phase is completed.

Providing Postcontract Services

The agent continues to represent the writer even after the writer and publisher have signed the contract. Once the publisher agrees to buy the book, the writer continues to revise it based on the editor's recommendations, and the agent may be involved in these exchanges. English notes that the agent may also assist the writer in the editing and polishing of the manuscript and help resolve any issues the author faces during the production process.

Other postcontract services vary depending on the agent and the needs of the writer. Agents assist in resolving any issues that occur between the writer and the publisher. "An agent can help if there are any problems that arise," says literary agent Jennie Dunham of Dunham Literary. "The agent also sells subsidiary rights that were retained by the author (audio, motion picture, commercial, etc.) and reviews royalty statements as they come in."[22] An agent may also make marketing suggestions to help increase the book's sales. If the publisher eventually stops printing new copies of the book, the agent can request that copyright be returned to the author.

Another important service agents provide is the handling of payments from the publisher. Agents serve as the collection and distribution point of advances and royalties for their writers. Publishers send the advances and royalties directly to the agents, who subtract their fees and send the balance to the writers.

Agent Income

In exchange for their services, agents can legitimately charge authors for certain expenses that have been agreed upon in advance. These fees include their commission and some direct costs of selling manuscripts, such as photocopying and postage expenses. What an ethical agent does not do is ask for money up front or charge for reading a manuscript. Such practices are prohibited by the Association of Authors' Representatives (AAR), a trade association for agents. The AAR's position is that charging reading fees is a "serious abuse that reflects adversely on our profession."[23] AAR membership is voluntary, and not all reputable agents join, but membership implies a high ethical standard.

A reputable agent, then, receives a percentage of what an author gets paid by a publisher. Typically, the commission is 15 percent of an author's advance and royalties. An agent may make a larger percentage on sales of subsidiary rights, which include selling the book in another country (foreign rights) or making it into a movie (dramatic rights). On average, literary agents make between $20,000 and $60,000 a year, with some agents' income exceeding $100,000.

How much agents earn can vary, depending on whether they work independently or for an agency, the number of authors they work with, the types of books they represent, and how well their clients' books are selling. Murphy says, "Some agents focus on quieter projects, others splashy bestsellers. I can tell you I sold 30 projects last year. Of course, what an agent makes doesn't just include advances on new projects; we continue to make 15 percent as a client's advance earns out and the book continues to generate royalties."[24]

Work Environment

If they work for an established literary agency, agents may receive a salary along with a share of the commissions. Lucy Childs, an agent with the Aaron M. Priest Literary Agency, feels that working for an agency has its benefits. "This agency's reputation precedes me, so I am able to take advantage of that," says Childs. "I also enjoy the camaraderie of a small group of highly intelligent and loyal people—all working towards the same goals and basically with the same interests."[25]

Another option for agents is to start their own business. Improvements in technology have made it easier for independent agents to run an office. Although solo agents have to undertake the risks that come with being business owners, they also keep the profits and have more control over their work life. For example, agents may choose to work from home or in an office setting. Working from home provides flexible hours and can help with child care arrangements. Many agents are located in the same cities as the major publishers, such as New York, but working in Manhattan is not a requirement for an agent.

Whether they work from home or in a downtown office, literary agents may not complete all their projects during typical work hours. Childs says that the official hours of the agency that she

Literary agents often work in the same cities where major publishers are located, such as New York City (pictured).

works for are 9:30 A.M. to 5:30 P.M., but that most of the agents work longer than that. Independent agent Grosvenor says that she reads most of her manuscripts at night and during off hours, since it is hard to find time during a typical day to actually read.

A Typical Day

A typical day for a literary agent is a busy one. It may include reviewing queries and submissions, contacting editors, negotiating contracts, working with writers to improve their manuscripts, researching markets, and following up on royalty or advance payments. Agents may also travel to attend conventions and writers' conferences, where they can learn about what is being published and meet with editors and potential clients. Murphy says,

> Today my to-do list included going through two new contracts, filling out some tax forms for a check that came from England, sending four manuscripts to an editor who asked to read them, coming up with a plan for where to send a new client's manuscripts, phoning an editor to confirm a rumor I heard about

a new area her company will be publishing in, and reading a novel by a writer who wants me to be her agent. And, of course, dealing with phone calls and emails as they come in.[26]

Besides the concrete tasks agents must accomplish, they also handle less tangible items. Grosvenor says, "An agent is a writer's broker, but he or she can be much more than that term implies. Personally, I see my role as agent as being that of editor, sales person, career builder, cheerleader and tireless advocate for the rights of my authors and their works."[27] The book *Literary Agents* by John F. Baker also mentions the various roles a typical agent performs. "Now that editors are for the most part much less nurturing of their writers . . . the agent is expected to be a combination of editor, psychologist and confessor, constantly available for consultation, advice, commiseration and congratulation."[28]

The AAR and Agent Ethics

Michael Congdon, a former vice president of the Association of Authors' Representatives (AAR), explains in an interview with the author the importance of the Canon of Ethics that AAR members are required to follow:

The AAR provides the image of fair practice and professionalism on behalf of its membership because to become a member, an agent must adhere to a code of ethics (the Canon of Ethics) and demonstrate professional competence to the Membership Committee and the Board of Directors before they are allowed to join. This image is critical because trust is probably the most important factor between agents and authors. . . .

The Canon of Ethics is important because of the professionalism and competence it demands. While not joining the AAR or adhering to the Canon of Ethics doesn't mean an agent is unscrupulous, there are those outside of the organization who have taken advantage of authors.

Required Agent Skills: Evaluating and Editing

How much nurturing an agent provides is often a matter of individual style, but there is no escaping the need for some editorial skill. The amount of editorial work performed varies, but an agent must be capable of judging a manuscript and making suggestions to improve it.

Some agents gain their editorial skills from prior work as editors; others learn on the job. Goldblatt, whose experience had been in negotiating rights rather than editing, says, "I work with a lot of authors in the editorial capacity, much more so than I ever thought I would, which required learning as I went along, because I wasn't an editor. But I know what I like. And I know when I read something what works and what doesn't."[29]

Communication

In addition to recognizing talent, the agent must effectively communicate with writers, editors, and publishers. Murphy feels communication abilities are the most vital skill for a good agent. "It can be delicate to communicate bad news to a client in a way that is also encouraging. Editors can be hard to get close to. Often I'm the 'bad cop' in a situation between a client and an editor, so their relationship isn't harmed by any particular situation—I work out the hard details with the editor."[30]

Communication is also the common element in almost all the tasks that English lists for a typical day. For example, she responds to queries and submissions from potential clients. She checks in with editors about current projects and new ones. She discusses topics like the marketplace, editorial comments, and promotional ideas with her existing authors.

Agents must also be adept at working with publishing contracts and understanding their terms as well as be proficient at negotiating on behalf of the writer. English says, "First, if the agent has represented the project in selling it, the agent will have to negotiate the major issues with an editor/publisher. Once the contract is issued, an agent will have to review each provision of the contract carefully to make sure all the agreed upon points are included and to see what other changes may be appropriate to better protect her author's interests."[31]

Agents must also be able to argue for the best possible terms for their clients, while maintaining a good relationship with the

A bookstore employee stacks copies of Colin Powell's autobiography. Working in a bookstore can be a good start for aspiring agents.

editors at the same time. The editors, after all, may be potential buyers of other projects from the agent in the future.

Entrepreneurial Skills

Besides being good communicators, agents who start their own businesses need to have entrepreneurial skills as well. *Literary Agents* by John F. Baker contains a series of agent interviews. In his introduction Baker summarizes that agents

> come from all sorts of backgrounds, but most of them started out with the same kind of urges and ambitions that take people into book publishing in the first place: a love of good writing, a passion for reading, an inclination to spend a life associated with books and their creators. . . . Almost all, however, have a disdain for organized corporate life, an entrepreneurial drive, and a determination to succeed on their own that takes them through the tough times that marked the start-up years of most of today's successful agents.[32]

The agents' level of entrepreneurial skill will often determine how far they will advance. Independent agents must have the financial resources to support themselves until their agencies produce income. Agents need to be comfortable networking for clients and they must be able to run their own offices proficiently. As entrepreneurs, agents must also have the discipline needed to be self-employed and must be comfortable with taking business risks.

Preparing for a Career as an Agent

Success as an agent comes from a combination of skills, but much of what needs to be known cannot be taught in a classroom. While many agents studied literature because they found it interesting, some agents say a literature degree is not required. "Most people have English degrees, but they aren't that useful,"[33] says editor-turned-agent Betsy Lerner. She feels that working at a bookstore provides practical experience, since it gives would-be agents a chance to learn what books are being published, how they are marketed, and who is buying them.

Agent Jennie Dunham of Dunham Literary notes that on-the-job training is how agents learn the most. "While there are publishing related courses in college and after, these aren't necessary," she says. "Publishing is still an apprentice-based business where new employees learn on the job from more seasoned agents."[34] Agent Pattie Steele-Perkins, founder of the Steele-Perkins Literary Agency, also recommends finding a mentor. "When I started in

An Agent's Ideal Day

Agents look forward to the success of their clients. Literary agent Janell Walden Agyeman describes her ideal day:

An ideal day, always, is to get a phone call from an editor, a film producer, or a foreign publisher telling me that they want to sign up one of my projects and then make me an offer! An ideal day might also include seeing enthusiastic reviews for a client's new book or learning that a book is selling very, very well in the stores. And, yes, an ideal day would include reading a terrific book or proposal from a new author and getting goosebumps because it's just that good!

this business [in 1989], I had a wonderful mentor. The young assistant editors she introduced [me] to then are now vice presidents of major publishers. She taught me everything from the basics on how to submit a manuscript to the art of the deal."[35]

Would-be agents can look for an internship within an agency or can start by working in publishing. Before becoming agents many people gain experience working as editors or in another part of publishing. For example, Goldblatt handled publishing rights and contracts for thirteen years before starting his own agency. Grosvenor worked for eighteen years both acquiring manuscripts and selling foreign and subsidiary rights. Less common is the route English, who is an attorney as well as a literary agent, chose. "Like myself, a number of agents have gotten into the business through the legal profession, but probably a larger group have actually worked as editors at publishing houses. . . . Working as an editor can probably provide the best insight into the business and the market as a whole," she says. "Essential preparation is reading, and more reading."[36]

Advice for Aspiring Agents

A passion for reading and a love of books are common among agents. But reading alone is not enough—the type of material being read is also important. Dunham says, "The best advice is to read, read, read. Figure out what area you like to read in, and become an expert in that area. The classics are important, but modern literature is also important because an agent doesn't sell classics, an agent sells new work."[37]

Besides a love of reading, anyone who wants to be an agent should want to work with books. "The most important thing about considering any career in publishing is a love of the written word. People who love books will find huge rewards in this business," says Murphy. "It's not usually a path to becoming rich, but it's a way to do what you love and get paid for it. Being a part of making a book come to life is tremendously rewarding, a way of sort of being immortal, as books live forever."[38]

Chapter 3

The Editor: Acquiring, Perfecting, and Producing Books

The title "editor" applies broadly to many different people involved in the publishing of a book. For example, an acquiring editor focuses on finding good manuscripts to publish. The developmental editor works with the author to revise and improve a manuscript. After these revisions have been completed, the copy editor corrects spelling, punctuation, and grammar, and checks for consistent references. The production editor manages the process of turning a manuscript into a bound book. In general, these editorial roles vary depending on the position, the publisher's style, and the publisher's size. At a small publisher, one person may perform several of these functions, and even at large publishers there may be some degree of overlap.

The Acquiring Editor's Role

Acquiring editors acquire, or purchase, material to be published. Their job is similar to that of agents, since both are looking for marketable manuscripts or proposals. Usually, an acquiring editor looks for specific types of manuscripts, such as young adult thrillers, middle grade biographies, or how-to books, for example.

To find suitable manuscripts acquiring editors network with writers at conferences and other events, receive manuscripts from agents, and work with their previously published authors. Many acquiring editors also read manuscripts from writers they have not requested material from, in the hopes of discovering a talented new writer. Agents and networking events are more productive sources of manuscripts—a common estimate from editors is that they publish less than one percent of slush pile materials.

Acquiring editors may also generate their own ideas and look for a writer to create a book based on those. For instance, an editor might read a published short story and approach the author

Editors like this one frequently consult reference manuals to help ensure that manuscripts conform to the style guidelines set by the publisher.

A Typical Day for Editor Arthur Levine

Arthur Levine is best known as the editor of J.K. Rowling's books about Harry Potter. He has also been working with some new picture book talents: Dan Santat (The Guild of Geniuses), *Carmela and Steven D'Amico* (Ella the Elegant Elephant), *and Ana Juan* (The Nighteater). *Here he describes a typical day:*

I divide my time into three areas of focus—the future, the present and the past. "The future" would be finding authors and illustrators to publish. The present would be helping those authors and illustrators refine and perfect the books on which we're collaborating. And the past would be making sure the books I've published find their audience.

The first area of focus ("the future") includes reading manuscripts, talking to my assistant and associate editor about books *they've* read, going to conferences, looking at portfolios and keeping current with what's being published elsewhere.

The second area ("the present") is where I read the manuscript with a pencil in my hand, making marks, and conveying my reactions to the author in a way that helps them figure out what work they need and want to do. It's talking with authors over the phone, hashing out ideas and working through blocks. It could also mean going over a book dummy [mockup] with an art director and coming up with feedback for the artist. In the latter stages of a book's production I will be proofreading to be sure no mistakes have been made as the book goes through its journey from manuscript to bound book.

The last area ("the past") involves a great number of conversations with our sales and marketing department, collaborating with them to create a plan for presenting each book to the world, and creating the excitement that we hope will build and spill over to the booksellers and librarians who will introduce our books to readers. This part of my job would also include participating in decisions about when to reprint a book, how to capitalize on a good review, and other crucial passages in a book's life. All of these things are part of a typical day, though I hope not all of them on any *given* day!

An acquisitions editor discusses the terms of an author's contract. The contract outlines the manuscript's due date, the author's royalty rates, and the publisher's rights to the work.

about creating a novel. Especially in the textbook business, acquiring editors look for writers—usually teachers or college professors—to produce books on topics they wish to publish. They plan the publisher's list of upcoming titles by anticipating what books teachers will need. Then they look for authors to write the textbooks.

The Acquisition Process

Once an editor has found a promising manuscript or book proposal, the acquisition process begins. The procedure varies by publishing house, the type of manuscript, and the seniority of the editor acquiring it.

Editors typically consult with others at the company and get feedback on the promising material. They may discuss the project with their bosses or people in the marketing and sales departments. In some cases they may ask the writer to revise a manuscript, even before offering a contract, based on their own opinions and on what others have to say. After the writer makes any requested revisions, editors may present a manuscript at an editorial meeting, or, in the case of a smaller publishing house, may send it directly to a senior colleague (such as the publisher) for approval. Acquiring editors may prepare a profit and loss analysis and must be prepared to discuss factors such as sales potential. If there is not enough support for the project, an editor will send the writer a rejection. If the project's merit is agreed upon, the editor will offer a contract to the writer, either directly or through the writer's agent.

After editors receive a detailed book proposal that they are interested in, they get bids from several printers and make a financial plan for the book. Based on that, they determine the advance and royalty schedules. At publishers like Scholastic, they will then ask for a commitment to support the book from Scholastic Book Clubs and Scholastic Book Fairs before deciding to acquire a book. It is not until all these pieces are in place that contract terms are negotiated with the writer.

Negotiating Contracts

Once an editor is ready to acquire the manuscript, contract negotiation begins. If the writer has a literary agent, the editor will work out the terms with that agent. Otherwise, the editor contacts the writer directly. Editors must negotiate such items as the advance, royalty rates, what rights the publisher is acquiring, and when the completed manuscript is due. Although an editor may have some say in these matters, often the final decision is up to a senior colleague at the company, and the editor's job is to persuade the writer (or agent) to accept the publisher's terms. If the writer or agent requests other contract revisions, the publisher's contracts department may get involved.

Additional Editor Responsibilities

Besides acquiring projects, experienced editors also help to plan future book lists. Kate Waters works as Scholastic's executive editor of nonfiction and reference books. As an executive editor at Scholastic, Waters plans book projects several years in advance. She "takes a broad look at the [nonfiction] genre, [and] informs the department of changes in children's taste and teaching."[39] She also mentors newer editors.

Some editors take on managerial tasks, which require them to divide their time. For example, Steve Meltzer of Dutton Children's Books says,

As managing editor, I wear two hats and so I split my days between the business side of the editorial group and actual editing. I usually use the mornings for correspondence with authors via letter and email. In the later part of the morning, I read emails and manuscripts, and in the afternoon, I might attend an editorial meeting to discuss manuscripts I feel are promising. I will also use the afternoon for line editing and reviewing sketches from illustrators. I also spend a good amount of time discussing projects with the design, production, marketing, and sales department. Bookmaking is a collaborative process that involves many people. [40]

The Developmental Editor's Role

Sometimes the acquiring editor's involvement in a project ends after the contract is negotiated and signed. In this case a developmental editor helps shape and refine the book. Developmental editors may

A team of production editors meets to critique cover photo choices for projects they are working on. Creating books is a highly collaborative process.

recommend big-picture changes, like altering the content of the book, and they may suggest more detailed sentence structure and wording changes. Freelance editor Carol Barkin explains,

> All the various editing terms—developmental editing, line editing, substantive editing—are kind of flexible. In general, they mean working with an author on the structure and content of a piece, looking at whether it is logical and makes sense, whether it is interesting and exciting for readers, whether the plot (for fiction) or the organization (for nonfiction) is complete and satisfying, and whether the style is interesting, appropriate, and consistent—in other words, helping the author turn it into a good book. [41]

In many cases the same editor who acquires the manuscript also works to develop it. For example, Nina Kooij, as the editor in chief at Pelican Publishing, acquires and develops proposals and manuscripts. Kooij says, "An editor corrects writing so that it is ready for the reader. An edited manuscript can look like a student report, with the teacher writing corrections and questions on it. Today, I will review book ideas. . . . I will attend an editorial board meeting, where we will discuss the proposed manuscripts we've read. . . . I will also work on editing a manuscript that we have already contracted for publication." [42]

The developmental editor's role can differ depending on the type of book. Alice Pope is managing editor of the Market Books department at F&W Books. Since 1992 she has been the editor of the annual *Children's Writer's and Illustrator's Market*. Because the guide is an annual compilation of market data and related information, each year Pope oversees the articles and interviews that are included.

At textbook publishers the developmental editor arranges for book reviews by experts in the field or by people who teach the subject. The editor then summarizes the reviews for the author.

If the project is a picture book, another part of the developmental editor's job is to hire illustrators. In addition, these editors manage a writer's progress and maintain schedules for the book. They may also appraise the writer's work at certain points along the way. After the book is fully developed, the next editor to review it is the copy editor.

A developmental editor makes changes as she pores over a manuscript to ensure that the writing is logical, consistent, and interesting.

The Copy Editor's Role

The developmental editor's role is to make certain a book meets the needs of the market, but that does not mean it is ready for publication. It is the copy editor's job to be concerned with the line-by-line details of a book. Copy editors focus on misspellings, punctuation mistakes, and grammar problems. They check for consistent references and details, such as a character's blue eyes on page two not becoming brown on page ten. Copy editors also make sure the manuscript follows the publisher's "house style," rules such as how foreign words are spelled and whether certain words are abbreviated (such as *U.S.* versus *United States*).

Teresa Hudoba has been freelancing as a copy editor, indexer, and proofreader since 1989. She says, "Copy editors may also read text to improve style, which may mean deleting unnecessary words, substituting new words for incorrect or awkward ones, and rearranging sentences within paragraphs. Copyediting does not normally include fact-checking, but copy editors may be asked to do so on occasion."[43]

Copy editors need to walk a fine line, because they have to make sure manuscripts are correct without changing the writer's tone or intent. Barkin adds, "The best copy editors make a manuscript flow smoothly and clean up all the problems and errors while maintaining the author's 'voice' and without imposing a style or diction that is different from the author's."[44]

A Detailed Look at the Copyediting Process

Although each copy editor may approach a project differently, they generally start by checking the manuscript to make sure it is complete and that all the pages and any photos, tables, or illustrations are included.

Fact Checkers

A fact checker works to ensure that a book's content is accurate. Since one wrong detail can create doubt about an entire book, the fact checker's job is an important one. Kristi McGee, a freelance editor who specializes in children's books, describes the role:

A fact checker must first identify the facts that need to be checked, and then verify them with reputable sources. A common-knowledge fact, such as "July 4th, 1776, is the anniversary of America's independence from England," does not need to be checked. However, a more obscure fact, such as "Lorraine Hansberry published *A Raisin in the Sun* in 1959," does need to be checked—first for the spelling of the author's name and correct title, second that she is indeed the author, and third the publication date.

When checking such facts, it is important to evaluate the quality of the sources, especially when using the Internet. For something like this, I would go to the New York Public Library website to start. . . . Often, publishers will request that fact checkers provide at least one print source for each fact. Sometimes only one source is needed, but often two sources are suggested.

Then a copy editor begins reading. Hudoba says,

I frequently refer to dictionaries and reference books (print and online) to check spelling and usage of words and phrases, and to make sure that the text follows the style guidelines set by the publisher. I keep a style sheet of my own —a page of notes, sorted alphabetically, to track decisions about style and usage. For example, under 'N,' I may have a note regarding numbers "spell out larger than ten." . . . I mark changes as needed on the manuscript pages, and write notes on Post-its to the author or publisher to draw their attention to questions or comments. [45]

Copy editors can also edit documents electronically, so that their notes are contained within the computer file.

The Production Editor's Role

The copyediting phase is supervised by the production editor. Production editors also direct the other details that go into the process that transforms a manuscript into a book. In addition to overseeing copyediting, they manage big-picture items, like the book's schedule, and handle the detailed aspects of the editorial production process, such as checking page proofs and artwork. Production editors also have to monitor production costs, while still ensuring the book's quality.

Jennifer Strada, a senior production editor for trade children's books at Simon & Schuster, explains that after pages are proofread and corrected, and the artwork is changed if necessary, then the production editors "check revised pages, with revised artwork—and will continue this cycle until final pages are approved. At that point, we send a set of final pages and a disk to the printer. The printer sends proofs for approval. After the book is printed, we receive samples of the bound books—and we inspect them to make sure that they look perfect." [46]

Production editors need to interact with a number of people throughout the production process. They often hire and supervise the work of freelancers, such as copy editors, proofreaders, and indexers. They serve as the go-between for the editorial, design, and production departments, communicating with each area as needed. Typical tasks might include "copyediting manuscripts; evaluating artwork; checking page proofs; inspecting bound books;

A production editor reviews page proofs. Production editors manage the process of transforming manuscripts into published books.

monitoring schedules; e-mailing book teams about project status," according to Strada. "It's a fast-paced work environment with lots of creative people,"[47] she says.

A Typical Day

Working with creative people is typical for editors. The exact tasks performed during an average day depend on whether the editor focuses on acquiring, developing, copyediting, or producing a manuscript. Editors may read and revise contracted manuscripts, correspond with writers, illustrators, agents, and other editors, and work with book designers. An editor's day may also include reviewing sketches and art for books, writing catalog and jacket copy, assembling information for the sales, marketing, and publicity departments, and planning production schedules.

Editors may have to edit books on topics that do not necessarily interest them. Leland F. Raymond, coauthor of *Orion the Skateboard Kid* and founder of CyPress Publications, points out that as an editor "you don't always get to pick the types of editing jobs you'll be working on. Whether you're editing a manuscript for a college physics professor or a novice fiction writer or an accomplished poet, each manuscript poses challenges as unique as the person who wrote it."[48]

Regardless of the topic, making a book come to life is one of the main rewards of the job. Kate Gale, the managing editor of Red Hen Press, says the best part is "when you work with a manuscript that really is great but needs carving, and after a few months it emerges, like [Michelangelo's statue of] David emerged from a chunk of marble, in all its awful beauty, and you helped make it happen."[49]

Work Environment

Editors can help to bring books to life in two work environments: working for a publisher or performing editorial roles on a freelance (project) basis. Most publishers have standard business hours, such as 8:30 A.M. to 5:00 P.M., but hours can increase as book deadlines approach, and many editors do their manuscript reading outside of the office. They often read during evenings and weekends and use their office time for other editorial tasks.

Book editing is a job that is especially suitable for freelancers. Starting out as a freelancer can be easier if the editor has worked for a publisher first. Working as a freelancer gives editors more freedom to choose their projects, but also involves finding clients. Marketing and networking are important aspects of a freelancer's business. Barkin says,

> Many freelance editors work for publishers—they get work from the people they used to work with on staff, from others they know in the business, from editors who hear about them from other editors. Freelance editors also advertise in various magazines and journals that are read by publishers and authors and add their names to directories published by various organizations. The Editorial Freelance Association offers job listings and other contacts to its members.[50]

Freelance editor Kathleen Erickson, who started her own business, Erickson Editorial, says that there are pros and cons to freelancing:

> Freelance advantages are that you are your own boss, you set your own work schedule. You get to work at home, which is

comfortable and fun. The disadvantages are that you work alone *a lot* and you have to like that. . . . Also, you have to keep looking for work all the time and manage saying no when you have too much to do. And you worry about having not too much work at one time and not too little. Another disadvantage is that you don't get a pension or insurance or paid days off. But the advantage is freedom.[51]

Salary Information

A freelancer's income level is more uncertain than an editor who works for a publisher. Editors' salaries differ depending on the size of the publisher, the publisher's location (with higher income earned in major cities), and the editor's level of experience. According to the U.S. Department of Labor, the median annual salary for editors in book publishing was about $40,000 in 2002.

Publishers Weekly conducts an annual survey of its subscribers. According to its 2003 survey of 563 people, editorial assistants made between $28,000 and $31,000 (depending on the size of the publisher). Editors earned between $41,000 and $61,000. Salaries increased for senior editorial positions.

Freelance rates can vary based on the type of editing, the timeframe for completion, and any special knowledge needed (for example, for scientific materials). The Editorial Freelancers Association indicates that developmental editors can charge from $32 to $60 for one to five manuscript pages (an hour's work). WritersMarket.com describes hourly copyediting rates as $17 at the low end (for light copyediting of general material), $50 at the high end, and $75 per hour as very high (for substantive copyediting of more involved text, such as technical material). Freelance production editors can charge from $15 per hour at the low end to $75 at the high end, with $150 per hour being very high.

Preparing for a Career as an Editor: Skills Needed

Although their incomes can vary, acquisition, developmental, copy, and production editors all share a love of books and reading. They know good writing, they know what makes it good, and they enjoy making it even better.

A freelance editor works from home. Freelancers are able to set their own hours, but they must meet the client's deadlines.

Acquiring editors must be able to judge a manuscript's potential, and developmental editors need to determine what changes would improve it. Acquiring and developmental editors must be good at maintaining their relationships with authors and editors, both of whom may be sources of future projects.

Copyediting requires excellent language skills. "I think most good copy editors are people who love words and language," says Barkin, "who speak grammatically themselves, who 'hear' errors in grammar and know instinctively how to fix them, and for whom errors in spelling and grammar stick out in a page of type."[52] Copy editors also need curiosity and patience to read and correct various types of manuscripts.

Production editors need to pay attention to details, and like other types of editors, they need to have strong writing and editing skills. Because they deal with scheduling and coordinating deadlines with other departments, these editors must be flexible and organized.

The Young to Publishing Group: Networking for the Newly Hired

To help newly hired and entry-level publishing employees to network with others in the industry, the Association of American Publishers (AAP) started the "Young to Publishing Group" (YPG). In 2004 YPG had six hundred members across various publishing houses and departments. Anne Garinger is the AAP project manager and staffs the YPG. She provides human resource departments at the publishing houses with YPG information so that new hires learn about it as soon as possible. It also gains members from word of mouth. Garinger says, "YPG members meet other people new to the industry and have the opportunity to develop a professional network." The YPG sponsors monthly lunches with guest speakers, creates a quarterly newsletter, and organizes various social events.

Waters notes that editors are only one piece of the publishing process. "An editor is a team player," she says, adding,

> Behind each book is not only the author and the editor, but equally important people such as art directors, designers, copy editors, proofreaders, people who buy the paper the book is printed on, people in the warehouses where books are packed, and librarians and booksellers who make sure that kids are introduced to good books. If a young person likes to read, and appreciates words, and is a team player, then publishing is for her. [53]

Education and Training

Due to the range of skills needed, editors can come from a variety of disciplines, such as history, communications, education, religion, and the sciences, although English majors are certainly common. While a few schools, such as Purdue University, offer a "Writing and Publishing" major, publishing degrees are more common at the graduate level. Several nondegree programs are also available for college graduates, such as the Columbia Publishing

Course (formerly known as the Radcliffe Publishing Course) and various certificate programs.

Because of the popularity of editorial jobs and the high level of competition to get them, students should prepare by gaining as much experience as they can. This can come from working on the school newspaper, tutoring other students in English and grammar, or starting their own newsletter. At the college level, students can apply for publishing internships so that they gain knowledge by working in the field.

Many nondegree programs are open to would-be editors. Columbia University in New York, for instance, offers a publishing program to college graduates.

Advice for Aspiring Editors

Strada notes that job satisfaction can be higher if editors are working with the type of books they love. When choosing a first publishing job, she advises, "think about what kinds of books you'd enjoy working on, and try to find a beginning-level job working on those books. Then from there you'll gain experience and can learn and grow while working on books that inspire you."[54]

Because books are the key product in publishing, "Read!" is common advice for would-be editors. Kooij says, "My advice is not only to read voraciously and widely but to pay attention to what you're reading—the construction of the sentence, the patterns of punctuation, the proper use of words, spelling, etc. You can learn even more about proper writing this way than through classes."[55]

Whether editors acquire, develop, copy edit, or produce books, they all make significant contributions to a book's creation. They share the common goal of making each book the best it can be.

Chapter **4**

The Book Designer: Crafting the Book's Appearance

Book designers are responsible for crafting a book's appearance. Their goals are to create a cover that sells the book and to lay out the interior so that readers can easily understand its contents. For example, they plan the cover, determine the margin size, select the typeface, decide the font sizes, and lay out any interior artwork or photos. "The design of books is much more than how a book looks, it is how a book works," says John Reinhardt, founder of John Reinhardt Book Design. "I do for books what an architect does for buildings. I determine how a book should look. . . . My ultimate task is to bring the author and reader together one-on-one."[56]

Book-Design Roles

Book designers and art directors are both involved with the design process. The specific job responsibilities for these roles can differ depending on the publishing house. Sometimes the designer is responsible for the interior of the book, and the art director is in charge of creating the cover and managing the overall design

A designer at Harlequin Books creates a cover with the help of his computer. Designers are responsible for conceiving a book's overall design.

process. For example, Cartwheel Books, the division of Scholastic that produces the *Clifford the Big Red Dog* series, has used this model. When the design and art director roles are separate like this, the art director typically hires illustrators, plans the book's cover, and supervises the design process. By contrast, "a designer has more of a hands-on role, placing art and text together in the mechanicals [the final design version] to create the book," says Edie Weinberg, the former senior art director of Cartwheel Books and the Scholastic Book Group. "The designer will show the AD [art director] layouts that they discuss and perhaps the AD will ask the designer to make adjustments. . . . The size of the [book] list the AD manages is what determines how much hands-on design the AD can handle. Some may choose to design the more high-profile books on their list." [57]

At publishers such as Harlequin, the book designer works as a partner with the art director. After discussing various concepts and styles for a book with the editorial and marketing departments, the designer creates an exterior and interior design, and the art director looks for illustrators or photographers to execute the cover.

Another possibility, particularly at smaller publishers, is that the designer and the art director are a combined role performed by one person. Christian Fuenfhausen, who works as both the designer and art director at Milkweed Editions, aptly points out that "job titles can be murky sometimes."[58] Regardless of the precise job title, people in design create the book's cover, the interior, and may be responsible for additional marketing materials as well.

Designing the Cover

The most important design element for a book is its cover, since many consumers will make a decision to read a book based solely

A graphic designer reviews cover mock-ups. Arguably the most important element of books, covers typically undergo several revisions before being finalized.

on the way it looks. Prior to planning the cover, departments such as editorial, marketing, and design may meet to come up with a vision for the book. For example, editors contribute insight into the plot, the marketing team discusses the intended audience, and the art director or designer provides input about what type of graphics will work best. Based on this type of meeting, cover designers then come up with possible images and typography. Brian McGroarty, the design manager for Harlequin, explains,

> To design a good book you have to visually communicate the elements (hooks) of the story that will entice potential readers to pick it up. Once these elements have been established, the key is to execute them in a unique way. The use of art style, type (lettering), color and placement are key in creating an appealing package. Personally, I think type is the most underrated and crucial element on a cover.[59]

Designers will often create several different versions of a cover and then share them with the other departments. For example, after Christian Fuenfhausen gets information about the book and its marketing plan, he creates a few cover ideas. Then he presents them at a meeting of the editorial, marketing, and production staff. They may pick a design and ask for changes or select one as is.

In general, once the plan for the book's design is in place, the actual cover images can be created in-house or they may be outsourced to freelancers. Designers must balance an effective cover design with the cost of creating it. Commissioned original illustrations will be more expensive than an image created by the designer or one available for free. For example, Fuenfhausen designed a cover for *Presidential Powers* with no art budget. The book is about a section of the Constitution, and Fuenfhausen found a high resolution image online of the original Constitution for no cost through the National Archives. For his design of *Every War Has Two Losers*, which also had no art budget, he spent his own money to have dog tags created. A photo of the dog tags adorns the book's cover, which was created for under thirty dollars.

Due to marketing plans, the exterior and interior designs for a book are often on different schedules. For example, sales catalogs and other promotional tools may display the cover before the interior design is completed. McGroarty notes that at Harlequin covers are printed for use by the sales group about ten months before

A graphic artist lays out a book on his computer. The template he uses to set the book's interior was created by a designer.

the book's publication date. So on some occasions the cover is completed before the manuscript.

Designing the Interior

When it comes to the interior, however, designers must wait until the manuscript is finished and all the editing is done. Once the manuscript is complete, work on the interior design can begin. Dotti Albertine of Albertine Book Design says that a "clean, smart design feels so pleasurable to read that you would never know anyone has labored over it."[60] But book designers do labor behind the scenes over the way a book is arranged. They consider the book's content, the audience, and the publisher's style as they determine the book's layout. The cover design can also significantly influence the way the inside of the book looks. From the story's typeface to the page numbers, each design element is selected to contribute to the overall book.

Designers make many decisions about the inside of the book. They may start the interior design process by setting the margins. Next they decide on the typeface for the main text of the book.

They design each page of the front matter (the book's opening pages), such as the dedication page and the table of contents. They also design the back matter, including any index, bibliography, and glossary pages. They consider the placement of any photos or illustrations, the quality of the paper, and which font sizes to use. Depending on the sales goals and retail prices, some books such as mass market paperbacks will have a limited amount of interior design work.

Designers often choose to repeat typefaces to achieve continuity. The style of type used on the front cover may be repeated on the title pages and other places within the book, and the secondary type, used for the author's name on the cover, is repeated within the book as well.

Even seemingly trivial details like where to place the page numbers must be decided with care. If a page number is placed in the

The Importance of Math

John Reinhardt, the designer of more than thirteen hundred books, says, "Almost every element of book design requires some use of mathematics." For example, to find out how many pages a certain book will need, designers must factor in things like the line length, the number of lines per page, and the size of the characters. They must frequently convert between inches, picas, and points (units of typographic measurement: one inch equals six picas; one pica equals twelve points) in their design work.

Another way that designers use math is to size images. "This is important when you have a spread of several photos of headshots and the photos are of different sizes and perspectives," Reinhardt explains. "As a designer, you must be able to scale and crop the photos so the end result will be a consistent size of heads within the photos."

Computing margins and spacing, fitting the book within a specified number of pages, and determining spine widths all require calculations. "The design of every element on a text page is defined, in one way or another, [by] a mathematical equation. There is rarely a moment where math is not used in the building and production of a book."

outside margin and the printer does a poor job trimming the book, the effect could mar the book's appearance.

When the dozens of decisions about the book's interior have been determined, the designer creates a list of instructions for the typesetter, covering each detail of the book. Although the designer's work is not necessarily obvious, the result should be a book that is easy to follow even if the content is complicated.

Managing the Illustration Process

Another part of the book-design process is the hiring and managing of illustrators. This is particularly important for children's picture books where the artwork is as critical as the text. Art directors receive samples from prospective illustrators on an ongoing basis, and they may contact artists whose work they have noticed in magazines. The editor and art director may work together to select just the right illustrator for a project. Once the artist is chosen, the art director negotiates the details of the assignment, such as the number of illustrations and the deadline for their completion.

After illustrators are hired, art directors manage the creative process by reviewing sketches and page layouts and then sharing the results with the editors. Executives as well as sales and marketing people may check the sketches while the book is in progress. They may request changes, such as the way a character looks. The art director is responsible for giving the illustrator any feedback.

Designers may also be involved in creating promotional materials to help sell the books. For example, they may design posters for the bookstores to display and advertisements for newspapers and magazines. Because of the costs involved, these types of materials may be produced only for books with high potential sales.

Working for a Publisher

Designers can do these tasks in two types of environments. They can be directly employed by a publisher, or they can freelance on a project-by-project basis. Helen Robinson, for example, is the art director for Front Street Books. As the art director for a small publisher she is involved with all phases of the book's design. "When you pick up a Front Street book," she says, "everything about the way it looks and feels is because I designed it that way." She works with four other people: the publisher, two editors, and a marketing

An editor and graphic artist at a small publishing company review art choices for book covers.

director. "We work very closely and exchange ideas about every aspect of the work. We have fun working together because we all love what we do and really like each other." [61] By comparison, an art director at a larger publishing house may work in a bigger design department with a couple of full-time designers and several freelancers.

Publishing house book designers typically work during the regular business hours for that company. For example, Fuenfhausen usually works 9:00 A.M. to 5:00 P.M. During seasonal deadlines and other crunch times, however, he may put in longer days. McGroarty notes that at Harlequin tight deadlines can mean longer hours. "In our department, you can usually find someone between seven in the morning until nine at night," he says. "There are occasions when deadlines may dictate working around the clock to complete an important project." [62] A designer's need to work occasional overtime is fairly common.

Working as an Independent Designer

Independent book designers are also subject to working longer hours during crunch times. These designers work for a variety of clients: authors who self-publish, small publishing companies, and large publishing houses. Publishing houses may use freelancers if their current staff is overbooked or if they need a certain style that would be created more effectively by an independent designer. At larger firms the production manager typically hires the freelancer.

Freelance designers usually work from a home office. They set their own hours and can avoid the meetings that an in-house designer must attend. Albertine says, "I love the freedom of working at home. My office is in my loft in Santa Monica [California]. I can see the sea from my window. If I want to work late on a project I can work until 2 A.M. If I want to run down to the beach for an hour walk, I can go when I want, then come back to work."[63]

Some freelancers feel that being self-employed increases their level of creativity. Reinhardt says,

> I am not limited to the style or the process of a publisher. I have found that being employed as a "house designer" requires a considerable level of conformity, which stifles creativity. . . . Working for a publisher also limits the contact I have with the authors. I like working with a variety of people and on a variety of books. Working for myself allows me to choose the books I wish to do and the people with whom I wish to work.[64]

Independent designers must invest in their own computer equipment to do the job. For example, Albertine has two computers, a backup drive, a scanner, a large format printer, a regular printer, and a fax machine.

Freelancers must also decide how much to charge and must take care of their own billing. Like other freelancers, freelance designers do not receive a regular paycheck, so their income can be uncertain. Reinhardt points out that it can take a while to build up enough clients to produce significant earnings. "Being an independent book designer is an extremely specialized profession," he says. "It is not one you can just walk right into. It takes a long time to develop a client list that will provide enough work to make a decent living."[65]

Since independent designers are self-employed, they must also seek out work. They must continually market themselves and network for new clients. Independent designer Susan Newman says that in addition to managing her existing design projects, she looks for new work each day. She points out that designers also need to keep their logo, Web sites, and promotional materials updated so that clients get a sense of their style. Marketing is an ongoing task on a freelancer's list of things to do.

A Typical Day

Whether they work on staff for a publisher or are freelancers, designers juggle different projects that are at various stages in the publishing process. For an art director a typical day may include meeting with an illustrator, reviewing sketches, and routing different phases of the book to different people as needed. As an art director/designer, Fuenfhausen's to-do list includes "generating sample pages for a book of poetry, finishing a seasonal catalog design, [and] completing two final paperback type proofs of covers." He then circulates the covers for in-house approval before creating a color proof and sending it to the printer. He also writes "ridiculously exacting typographic specifications for the typesetters"[66] so they know how to format the pages for printing. A designer may also be responsible for coordinating the necessary details with the printer for the book's production.

An independent designer's day may include responding to requests for estimates, contacting clients about proofing certain phases of the design, and handling billing and other small business responsibilities.

For both staff designers and freelancers the typical day can be a rewarding one. Albertine says,

> I love being a book designer because I love books. It is so much more gratifying than basic advertising design to me, because I get involved in each book, and learn about so many different things in the process. . . . The down side is that unless you own the publishing company, you'll probably not make tons of money. However, one can earn a nice livelihood utilizing one's creativity while having your brain stimulated with fascinating subjects.[67]

The Illustration Process

Lena Shiffman has illustrated a number of books, including Dancing with the Manatees *and* When I Lived with Bats. *This is the process she goes through after being hired to illustrate a picture book:*

I first read the manuscript to get an overall feel for the story. Then I read it again, but this time I start sketching. I break the book up into how many pages it will have and make a storyboard. . . .

In my storyboard I draw very rough sketches, since it is only a guide for me. . . . I ask myself: What is the most important part of the story to illustrate? How do I show that? What angle would make this more interesting? . . . Leaving enough room for the text is very important and is also part of the overall design of the page.

After the storyboard, I head to the library for research. . . . I need to have pictures of the animals I am illustrating to make sure I draw them accurately. . . . Since a lot of my stories have people in them too, I do use models. . . . I used my husband when I was doing the book *Listening to Whales Sing*. He was supposed to be the marine biologist and I wanted him to pose, pretending he was on a boat in the middle of the Atlantic Ocean just about to dive into the water to take pictures of a humpback whale. He was really on our coffee table in our living room. . . .

When all my research is done, I will start sketching each page of the book. . . . By this time, the art director has sent me galleys of the text, which is the text in the right font and size as it will be in the book. I cut the text out and paste it onto [copies of] my art where I have left room for it. I then glue each page together and make a book dummy. . . . I send this to the publisher so they can see how I see the book and if we have the same vision. Being an illustrator is being part of a team. . . .

When the dummy is returned to me, I first make the corrections [if the art director made any] and then I start painting. . . . I trace each drawing onto my watercolor paper using a light table. After each illustration is painted, I send them off to the publisher. I usually have to wait about six to twelve months before I get the finished book. . . . It is always exciting to see the finished product after such a long time. It makes it look all new to me again and if I like it I dance around the house.

Salary Information

To determine how much designers earn, the American Institute of Graphic Arts (AIGA) together with a company called Aquent conducts an annual survey about design professionals and their income. According to the 2004 AIGA/Aquent Survey of Design Salaries, the median nationwide compensation was $30,000 for entry-level designers (categorized as those who have been out of school for one to two years) working specifically at publishing houses. The median for publishing house designers (not entry-level) was $37,500. For senior designers the median increased to $54,000, and for art directors it rose to $70,000.

Necessary Designer Skills

In order to succeed in this field aspiring designers need to be able to produce visually interesting ideas. "A good sense of aesthetics, color, love of solitude, and the joy of putting words and shapes into form"[68] are all important, says Albertine.

A graphic designer arranges a layout on a light table. Creative designers are able to produce images that are highly appealing to the reader.

Due to the calculations involved in laying out the book's interior, designers also need to be detail oriented and proficient in math. Weinberg points out that other abilities, such as organization and management skills, are necessary as well.

Because they are their own supervisors, and because they must find their own clients, self-employed designers need discipline as well as marketing and networking expertise to succeed as entrepreneurs. Newman says that independent designers must also be good at researching the client, the topic, and the competition, "so your designs are not only appropriate but stand out from the crowd."[69]

The ability to work as part of a team is essential in producing a book. Designers also need to be good listeners, because miscommunications can waste everyone's time. The designer needs to clearly understand what authors, editors, and marketing people are looking for in a design.

Computer skills are also required, because computers allow designers more flexibility and make it easier to experiment with an object's placement and size. While computers are important as tools, Brian McGroarty stresses that technology alone cannot make someone a good designer. "Learn how to use a pencil!" he says. "Computers don't create great designs, people do!"[70]

Preparing for a Design Career

To learn how to create those great designs, many book designers and art directors studied subjects such as fine arts or graphic design in college. In a 2002 survey by *How* magazine of more than five hundred designers working in various fields, 85 percent of those under the age of thirty had a design degree.

Over fifty colleges in the United States offer a major in design and visual communications. In graphic design programs students learn about the use of color, proportion, symmetry, and type design. They may take classes in visual communication and typography, for instance. Design programs may also include training on specific computer software such as Quark and Photoshop.

Reinhardt recommends that future designers learn about all the areas involved with book publishing, including writing, editing, designing, printing, distributing, and selling. He feels that understanding the overall process benefits the designer.

McGroarty, however, says that good designers do not need to be educated in book design as long as they are good designers in general. Of his seven designers, only one studied book design specifically.

Students can learn about design by working on their school newsletter or yearbook and taking drawing, art, and desktop publishing classes. Web sites, such as the AIGA's, can also provide resource sections specifically for students.

Mentoring

Another way to become adept in this field is to work with a mentor. When new designers are mentored, they learn from the experience of someone in the field who is willing to teach them. This

Book Design: A Brief Example

The nature of the book itself can influence its design. "The goal is to create a harmonious and integrated whole," says designer Christian Fuenfhausen in an interview with the author.

For example, he designed the nonfiction book *Bird Songs of the Mesozoic* in 2004. The book is "intended to be a quirky 'Day Hiker's Guide,' and its cover sports an eccentric piece from a local artist," he explains. "So it was important that every design element reflect this quirkiness, including the type for the main body text." He experimented with different fonts to keep with the theme. "The type selected, and its size and leading [the blank space between lines] are crucial to whether the book will be enjoyable to read or will tax the reader."

After picking the main text font and making other design decisions, he created sample pages for the editors to review. He incorporated the editors' suggestions, then created typographic specifications, or specs. "It is a recipe of how to typeset the book. Every detail, no matter how small, must be covered. Once this is finished, we send the type specs, sample pages and the manuscript to the typesetters. . . . This is essentially the end of the design process" (although he continues to monitor the book during production).

is one way to supplement a formal education with practical hands-on knowledge. "I believe, like many professions, it is important to study with and learn from other book designers. To be a good designer, one must learn from a good designer," Reinhardt says. "A successful book designer will be one who has experienced all the functions of book production. Therefore, apprenticing or gaining a mentor in the book production field would be the first step to a career in book design."[71]

Advice for Aspiring Book Designers

Fuenfhausen advises future designers to observe designed items all around, "from the tags on your clothes, to . . . food packaging, restaurant signage and menus. . . . You start to see there's art work everywhere, and once you start seeing that or looking for it you can start deciding whether something 'works' and why."[72]

On a similar note, McGroarty stresses the importance of asking why. "When you see a fantastic design for anything, don't ask yourself, 'How did he do that?' [Instead] ask, 'Why did he do that? 'Why' is the creative, [while] 'how' is the execution. Both are important but without the 'why,' you just have a pretty picture."[73]

Overall, the goal is a successful design, but designers may need to alter how they define their accomplishments. "A successful design is not necessarily one that is the prettiest or coolest, but one that works well with all of the people and events involved," Reinhardt says. "If the success of the book hinges on getting it to press tomorrow, one must be able to create a quick and useful design to meet that deadline. It may not be your best work, but it satisfied the requirements presented. That is a successful book design."[74]

Chapter 5

The Sales Representative: Getting Books to Readers

Sales representatives are a vital link in the chain that begins with the writer and ends with the reader. Their jobs can vary based on whom the reps work for and who their clients are. In-house and commissioned sales representatives sell primarily to independent bookstores. Key accounts or national accounts managers focus on major buyers such as Borders or Barnes & Noble. An educational sales representative sells to schools, colleges, and libraries. A special sales representative sells to corporations, gift shops, and other nontraditional outlets.

Sales Representatives

Most children's books and adult hardcover books are sold primarily by bookstores. These stores are the sales representatives' primary customers. Sales people may work for the publisher directly, selling only that publisher's books (as an in-house or house rep), or they may work for a distributor selling multiple publishers' books (as a commissioned rep).

Most small and midsize companies rely primarily on commissioned reps, and the larger publishers may use at least some commissioned reps. In-house reps typically work for the larger publishing houses, but there are some exceptions. For example, Pelican Publishing, a midsize company, uses eight in-house reps exclusively.

Whether they work for a publisher or for a distributor representing many publishers, sales reps contact bookstores about upcoming books and provide information about publishers' new titles. Commissioned reps tend to travel more and meet buyers face-to-face. Because of cost constraints, most in-house reps contact their buyers by phone, but this varies by publishing company. The reps discuss what quantities the store may need and process the book orders. In addition to selling upcoming books, sales reps are also responsible for managing the backlist—that is, previously published books. Rebecca Fitting, a sales rep for Random House, says that there is an increasing focus on backlist books. Along with new books, she provides information about previously published books at each sales call, and may make separate sales calls focusing exclusively on backlist books.

Besides selling upcoming and backlist books, sales reps have other tasks as well. Roger Saginario, a sales rep for the Time Warner

Sales representatives inform bookstores of upcoming titles. Certain sales representatives known as national account managers handle major buyers such as Barnes & Noble.

Book Group, says, "Other responsibilities include [providing] customer service, managing the advertising programs that are offered, and communicating with your buyers about issues that may affect sales on certain books. An example might be notifying buyers that a particular author will be on TV soon to promote their book."[75]

Whether they are in-house or commissioned reps, salespeople usually cover clients in a specific geographical area. It may be small and densely populated, such as a borough of New York, or large and widespread, such as several states in the Midwest. Sales reps are also responsible for providing their publishers with sales reports on their assigned areas.

Educational Sales Representatives

Educational sales reps also work in regions. These types of reps sell textbooks and reference books to schools and libraries. As part of their job they may also search for potential authors to write books for the publisher. One college textbook sales rep says,

> As I see it, my two main responsibilities are to promote and sell our new books to professors and to [school] bookstore managers, and to encourage professors who are writing books to publish with us. . . . I don't think of myself as "working in sales"—rather I think of myself as working in educational publishing. As such, I feel that I'm contributing to the arena of students and professors who value books as integral to the learning process.[76]

Educational sales reps have a more defined target buyer than a rep selling popular fiction, for example. Jonathan David Morris, who sells college textbooks for Bedford, Freeman & Worth (BFW) says, "When it comes to academic publishing, you're pretty much guaranteed a customer base. Finding it is one thing, of course, but it can always be found so long as the title is strong and its style suits people's needs."[77] To find that customer, college sales reps analyze a school's course catalog and the school bookstore's current offerings to get a sense of where they can generate potential sales.

The National Accounts Manager

While educational sales reps sell to schools and libraries, the national accounts manager (or key accounts manager) focuses on the pub-

The Bookstore Owner's Perspective

Bookstore owners work firsthand with sales representatives. Linda Ramsdell, who has owned and operated the Galaxy Bookshop for almost twenty years, comments,

Because my store is small and in a rural, out of the way place, I have a mix [of types of reps]. I see a house rep from a few of the major publishers, have a phone rep for a few others, and order on my own from still other major publishers. I also see several commissioned reps representing smaller publishers.

The best sales reps really read the books on their list(s) and can speak articulately about them. They must also be able to build a trusting relationship with the booksellers. The very best reps have a passion for books that they can communicate to the bookseller. The result is the bookseller gets excited about a book and then communicates that to the customer, who communicates it to other readers, etc. etc. Passion may not be a skill, but I think it is the most important quality of a good sales rep. The skill is the ability to communicate the passion.

lisher's major commercial accounts, such as Borders and Barnes & Noble. This salesperson focuses on selling books to key accounts and troubleshooting any issues with them.

Celeste Risko is the national accounts manager for Little, Brown Books for Young Readers. She says,

I am the main liaison between the publisher I represent and the accounts which I serve, which means I not only present all the titles . . . to the buyers at some of the largest bookseller accounts in the country, but I also help resolve any problems those accounts have with any area of the publishing/ distribution world. . . . I help correct errors in listings and pricing. . . . By specializing in one subject area [children's books], I have been able to use that knowledge to greater effect in selling books to my accounts. They are aware that I am well versed in their business and I know that I can provide them with useful information.[78]

Special Sales

People who work in special sales (also called special markets) sell books to nontraditional outlets, such as mail-order catalogs, corporations, department stores, and gift shops. Special sales might include, for example, craft books to a chain of art stores, home improvement books to Home Depot, or decorating books to furniture stores. These types of sales expand opportunities for publishers beyond the traditional bookstore venue. Any nonbookstore that sells books is fair game for special sales. Bill Wolfsthal, director of specialty retail markets for publisher Harry N. Abrams, says, "Depending on the publisher and what kinds of books they publish, Special Sales can make up from 10 percent to 60 percent of a company's domestic sales."[79]

Businessmen browse through trade publications in a bookstore. Sales representatives must think like customers in order to market products appropriately.

With special sales, "books are ancillary [secondary to the store's main focus], so we are competing with other products for space," says Ron Davis, vice president of special sales at Sterling Publishing Company. "With that in mind, a sales rep has to be creative and forward thinking with their pitches." For example, Davis says, "They need to think like the customer. What are they [the customers] looking for? How can books complement an existing gift store or catalog? Will books help sell other products from the store or catalog?" [80]

The Sales Manager

After working in sales, depending on their interests and their previous sales performance, some reps become sales managers. Sales managers are responsible for hiring, training, and overseeing the other sales reps. Managers also supervise the reps' sales amounts, check the reps' sales against their goals, and may have sales accounts of their own.

"It's a combination of analysis and number crunching, determining what books are selling, what's not selling and why," says Joseph Billingsley, the sales manager at Pelican Publishing. "It's also a lot of hands-on management of the staff—coaching, motivating, putting out fires, working with them to brainstorm ideas to sell to their accounts. . . . I retain some accounts as well, and so I spend certainly several hours of the day actually selling to those accounts as well as managing the other folks." [81]

Sales Conferences: Knowing the Books

Both sales managers and sales reps need to be familiar with the books they are selling. Some publishing houses hold seasonal sales conferences to present their upcoming books to the sales force. These conferences can take place in person or via the Internet. At this point sales reps learn about the books they are expected to sell. Risko says, "We hear all about the books from the people who have been most intimately involved in their creation. They give us a brief description of the titles, we see whatever artwork is available at that time and learn all about the marketing and publicity plans for the titles. We also learn how many copies the publisher is printing and how much we, individually, are responsible for selling." [82]

Although the decision to publish a particular book has already been made, sales reps can still offer suggestions at sales conferences. For example, they might suggest a change in the color of the cover.

Not all sales conferences take place in person. "We have 'Webcasts,' where I stay at home with my headset on, an Internet connection, and the people from NYC congregate in one room at the NY office and present to us that way," says Simon & Schuster rep John Muse. "We listen to them speak, we have a software package that allows us to see book jackets (covers) as they are being presented, and we can ask questions by typing [them] into a 'chat room' or by speaking up via our headset."[83]

Publishers that do not hold sales conferences may supply their reps with a sales kit instead. The kit includes items such as catalogs, sales sheets, and sample books.

Knowing the Clients

Besides knowing the books, maintaining a strong relationship with each client is a key factor for a sales rep's success. It is only by meeting the needs of the buyers that sales reps can be successful. For textbooks, educational sales reps can research what books teachers currently use and be prepared to explain the advantages that their books offer. For bookstores, reps often become familiar with their needs by selling to them repeatedly over time. They can also learn by asking. Saginario says that meeting with bookstore owners or buyers is the best way to learn about their stores.

Making the Sale in Person

Because of the need to be close to the bookstores in their region, many salespeople work from home and travel to their sales calls. The amount of travel can vary throughout the year. In between their publishers' selling seasons, reps focus on preparation and following up with the bookstores' buyers. During busier selling periods, reps travel and make many face-to-face sales pitches. Muse describes a typical sales call as follows:

> Our "seasonal catalogs" . . . will have already shipped to the stores from the warehouse, so my buyers will have had the new catalogs for a couple of weeks or longer by the time I get there. A good many of my buyers will also have looked

In order to best meet the needs of their clients, sales representatives must get to know bookstore owners like this woman.

over the catalogs and put down initial order quantities for the titles.

I take a seat, open up my laptop and turn it on, and while this setting up process is going on, we chat about how they are, how the store is going, how my family or their family is, things of that nature. I visit with these folks at least three times a year, sometimes (with some customers) more often, so we know each other pretty well.

After about twenty to thirty minutes, we're ready to begin the process, and basically we open the first catalog (I usually give them the order of catalogs as we go along) and talk about each title, one by one. Many books are easy to figure out, that a store needs only one or two copies to start out, and sometimes we need to figure out whether the store needs three, five or ten copies of certain books. . . . We'll figure out together what that number needs to be for their store. Of course, I say "their store" because a store down on Cape Cod [MA] has different needs than a store based in Cambridge, MA—a tourist-oriented location versus a very strong college market store. . . . All in all, we're done in about three to four hours. [84]

Selling from a Distance

Not all sales reps meet the book buyers in person. Some conduct their sales by phone and e-mail. Morris, who sells textbooks, says, "It's pretty straightforward. When you have a new book, you get in touch with as many professors as humanly possible. . . . All of my pitches are made either by email or phone." [85]

Some salespeople work specifically as telephone sales reps (as opposed to field reps) selling trade books. Telephone reps are used for some of the smaller, more distant independent bookstores that have lower volumes.

A Typical Day

For reps who work from their home office by phone and e-mail, the hours are more regular. Some reps work typical eight-hour days. During busier sales season (for example, when new catalogs come out), hours may increase. In general, a sales rep with a home office needs a computer and fax as well as storage space for prepublication versions of the books that reps share with clients.

For salespeople who travel, the days can vary depending on the customers they are calling on. They may spend some days preparing for their sales calls, and other days visiting with clients. On travel days they may leave early to drive to a customer's location and then spend several hours with them. Some customers send in the orders later, others complete them on the spot. Reps may use laptops with software to submit orders instantly. They also participate in conference calls with their managers and other reps if they are not located near the publisher's office. During a busy selling season, they may put in fifty to eighty hours a week and spend many nights away from home.

In return for the travel, the job offers flexibility and independence. Working from home allows reps to structure their days in ways that best suit their needs. Muse says, "You can't beat working on your own. I don't go to the same place every day. I'm in my car for several hours each day, driving (most often) with the windows down and the sun shining. I like the mixture of solitude while driving and then meeting my customers. And while the emails do pile up, I do like getting home in the afternoon. I can help out around the house . . . and take care of that email at night if I want to."[86]

Selling Subsidiary Rights

Erika Bradfield works for Ten Speed Press in a different type of sales: foreign rights. Her work is based on what rights authors grant (or sell) to the publishers in their initial contract. For example, an author may grant mass market paperback rights, dramatic rights (for a motion picture), foreign, and/or translation rights. Bradfield says,

I give information on our titles to foreign publishing companies to see if they are interested in buying translation rights. Once I have sold one of our books to another publishing company, we negotiate the deal and I draw up a contract that states the terms of the agreement. I spend time talking with our authors who are always excited to see their books published in Japanese, or Turkish, or Polish. . . .

One of the most rewarding parts of my job is that I get to travel for the company. There are international book fairs that I attend in Germany and London each year. There are also many domestic book fairs where publishers, agents and subsidiary rights people gather to talk about books. I get to meet people from all over the world and interact with them. I really enjoy my job.

Working with Marketing and Publicity

Whether salespeople are conducting sales in person, by e-mail, or over the phone, effective marketing and publicity can help increase their sales. Publicists and marketing people help to create demand for the books that the sales reps are trying to sell. For example, the marketing department might create a floor display, posters, or other visual materials that help a book stand out. Prior to the holiday sales season, they may create a brochure that sales reps can use to highlight important books for the booksellers and their sales staff.

Lissa Warren, author of *The Savvy Author's Guide to Book Publicity* and senior director of publicity at Da Capo Press, says,

> It's a book publicist's job to get broadcast and print coverage of a book. Broadcast means on radio and TV. Print means in newspapers and magazines, and on websites. The idea is that the coverage makes people want to buy the book. Each week, I attend lots of meetings. Some of them are with the people I work with (the marketing director, the publisher, the editor, etc.). Some of them are with authors. Some of them are with the media to try to talk them into reviewing the book, or having the author on their show. . . . It's my job to get the media coverage, and it's our marketing director's job to make sure the sales reps, the bookstore buyers, and the consumer hear about the coverage.[87]

Salary Information

Maximizing sales through marketing and publicity is important to reps, since for most of them, their income is based on their sales performance. House reps typically receive a base salary plus a variable bonus that depends on their sales. Morris explains that at his company, "we have base salaries, but we don't receive direct commissions. Instead, we have two bonus periods, in which we start earning money the moment we exceed our sales goals. It's not an ideal way to pay for your house and support your family, quite frankly. . . . But it can also reap tremendous financial rewards for those who are patient with it."[88]

At some publishing houses the sales goal bonus is a combination of the sales rep's performance along with the company's sales success as a whole. If the company meets its sales goals, this sce-

Paul McCartney speaks to reporters during the 2001 release of his book of poetry. Effective publicity and marketing are integral to strong sales.

nario rewards sales reps for their efforts even if they do not meet the individual goals for their territories. House reps may also receive a company car, which some reps use to travel thirty-five to forty thousand miles a year.

Commissioned reps do not receive a base salary or a company car. Instead, they rely on commissions from their sales. Saginario points out that compared to field reps, commissioned reps will do better during good times but will do worse during bad times because their income is more variable.

According to *Publishers Weekly*'s 2003 survey of its subscribers, sales reps with less than three years' experience make about $50,000. Sales managers with over ten years' experience earn about $100,000. Sales managers receive a mix of salary and bonuses, according to Thomas Delano, who teaches the publishing marketing and promotion course for Emerson College's certificate in publishing program. The bonus amounts can range from 25 percent to 100 percent of the sales managers' salary, depending on their performance.

Success in Sales

To achieve a high level of income in sales, successful book salespeople need certain characteristics: They need to be personable, detail-oriented, organized, and good communicators, for starters. John Muse says,

> This position revolves around countless pieces of information—from the reading materials you get prior to the sales Webcast, to the packing of your car with the things you'll need on the sales call or the overnight trip, to the information you'll need to know to make the sales call successful. There are authors, dates, ISBNs [International Standard Book Numbers used to designate individual titles], print runs (the quantity of a book's first printing), marketing materials, prices, sales promotions. You need to keep track of it all in order to do the job well. [89]

As with other sales positions, sales reps must maintain a positive attitude when dealing with rejection. They must also be able to listen and communicate their points persuasively. It is not enough to just keep up with all the details. Good salespeople must also be able to share that information effectively with their potential buyers and with their managers.

For college textbook sales, one rep says, "[Selling college textbooks] is distinctive because of our market audience of college professors. We need to be well-versed in their disciplines and knowledgeable about our books. We need to be self-confident and enthusiastic and reliable and friendly and memorable and clever and service-oriented." [90]

Sales reps also need to be motivated and disciplined. Rebecca Fitting notes that a healthy work ethic is important for reps, since they are relatively unmonitored. Therefore, reps must be capable of working independently and getting the job done on their own.

Training and Education

While some attributes of a successful salesperson, such as work ethic, cannot be taught in school, students interested in working in sales can study a variety of majors such as English, communications, social sciences, accounting, business, and other business-related subjects. A few colleges offer sales-related continuing education courses as part of their publishing certificate programs. For example, the

Book Distribution

To comprehend what a salesperson does, it is helpful to understand the book distribution process. A book can reach the reader in a number of ways. Customers can purchase books through online retailers (like Amazon.com) and from some publishers directly. They can borrow them from a library, read them in school, or buy them from various retailers (such as bookstores, convenience stores, and gift shops).

A traditional route to a bookstore or library involves the publisher shipping the books to a wholesaler or distributor first. Although they are both intermediaries, wholesalers differ from distributors. In an interview, Josh Mettee, owner of the wholesaler American West Books, says, "Usually a distributor requires exclusive rights to sell the book . . . and receives a larger discount. The discount is large enough for wholesalers to actually purchase the books from the distributors. Distributors usually promote [books] and contact buyers, letting them know about new titles. Wholesalers generally don't do any promotions and just take orders."

Both wholesalers and distributors store the books until they receive orders for them. Then they transport them to the next point in the process (such as the retailer or a school). Mettee's wholesale company, for example, provides books to chain stores (like Barnes & Noble and Costco), smaller, local bookstores, and specialty stores like gift shops or museums.

Publishing

University of Chicago's Graham School of General Studies offers a Sales, Distribution, Marketing, and Publicity class and an Acquisitions and the Sales Force class. The Division of Continuing Education at Emerson College offers marketing and promotion coursework as part of its certificate in publishing program.

Reading widely is good preparation for a future book salesperson. Working part-time in a bookstore can also provide an aspiring sales rep with marketing and retail experience and a way to learn about the publishing business. Risko says,

> A job as a clerk in a bookstore is a great first job and would be an excellent way to determine if this business is right for you. You would experience selling to customers, learning about the marketplace, judging demand, marketing to the public, and gaining confidence on an interpersonal level. All of these experiences would stand you in good stead for a job on the other side of the business, which is selling to the companies that sell the books to you, the customer. [91]

Working in a bookstore is a great way for people to determine if a career in book sales is right for them.

Advice for Aspiring Sales Representatives

Working as a publishing house intern can provide students with insight into the industry and hands-on knowledge. Katura Hudson, an employee of Just Us Books says,

> Be sure to make the most of any other sales positions, or any other jobs you get. Show initiative. Ask to help with special projects. Develop your customer service skills. Seek out opportunities to practice speaking in public: sales people often have to give presentations to potential customers, and pitch products over the phone. Become proficient in computer programs such as Microsoft Excel and PowerPoint, both of which are used a lot in sales. [92]

As the publishing industry changes, the nature of sales jobs may change as well. Increased online sales and nonbookstore sales of books can affect the rep's future role. Random House sales rep Rebecca Fitting says, "This can be an exciting job, especially for someone young who likes to travel. There are constant changes in the field though, and my advice would be to never get too used to the way your job is, and to always be flexible. If you can't change with your job, your job will change without you." [93]

Notes

Introduction: Publishing: A Dynamic Industry

1. Quoted in Bob Minzesheimer, "10 Years of Best Sellers: How the Landscape Has Changed," *USA Today*, March 11, 2004, p. A01.
2. Quoted in Bradley J. Morgan, ed., *Book Publishing Career Directory*. Detroit: Gale Research, 1993, p. 3.

Chapter 1: The Writer: Creating Content

3. Quoted in Mary Smith, "What Is Success?" *Idaho Writers League Coeur d'Alene Chapter News and Views*, April 2002, p. 1.
4. Marcia Preston, e-mail interview by author, March 2004.
5. Stephen King, *On Writing: A Memoir of the Craft*. New York: Pocket Books, 2002, p. 166.
6. Kelly Milner Halls, e-mail interview by author, April 2004.
7. Deborah Hopkinson, e-mail interview by author, March 2004.
8. Anthony Tedesco, e-mail interview by author, July 2004.
9. Robin Friedman, e-mail interview by author, March 2004.
10. Elaine English, e-mail interview by author, May 2004.
11. Quoted in Jennifer Ferranti, "Grisham's Law," *Saturday Evening Post*, March/April 1997.
12. Preston, interview.
13. Sherry Garland, *Writing for Young Adults*. Cincinnati: Writer's Digest, 1998, p. 78.
14. Friedman, interview.

Chapter 2: The Literary Agent: Connecting Writers with Publishers

15. Deborah Grosvenor, e-mail interview by author, June 2004.
16. Barry Goldblatt, phone interview by author, March 2004.
17. Grosvenor, interview.
18. Goldblatt, interview.

19. Goldblatt, interview.

20. Erin Murphy, e-mail interviews by author, April and July 2004.

21. Elaine English, e-mail interviews by author, May and July 2004.

22. Jennie Dunham, e-mail interview by author, July 2004.

23. Association of Authors' Representatives, "Frequently Asked Questions," 2004. www.aar-online.org.

24. Murphy, interview.

25. Lucy Childs, e-mail interview by author, July 2004.

26. Murphy, interview.

27. Grosvenor, interview.

28. John F. Baker, *Literary Agents: A Writer's Introduction*. New York: Macmillan, 1999, p. ix.

29. Goldblatt, interview.

30. Murphy, interview.

31. English, interview.

32. Baker, *Literary Agents*, pp. x–xi.

33. Quoted in Sarah Tomlinson, "Job Q&A: Betsy Lerner," *Monster.com*, 2004. http://sales.monster.com.

34. Dunham, interview.

35. Pattie Steele-Perkins, e-mail interview by author, September 2004.

36. English, interview.

37. Dunham, interview.

38. Murphy, interview.

Chapter 3: The Editor: Acquiring, Perfecting, and Producing Books

39. Kate Waters, e-mail interview by author, April 2004.

40. Quoted in Robin Friedman, "Steve Meltzer, Managing Editor, Dutton Children's Books," *RobinFriedman.com*, 2004. www.robin friedman.com.

41. Carol Barkin, e-mail interview by author, May 2004.

42. Nina Kooij, e-mail interview by author, March 2004.

43. Teresa Hudoba, e-mail interview by author, May 2004.

44. Barkin, interview.

45. Hudoba, interview.

46. Jennifer Strada, e-mail interview by author, August 2004.

47. Strada, interview.

48. Leland F. Raymond, e-mail interview by author, August 2004.

49. Kate Gale, e-mail interview by author, March 2004.

50. Barkin, interview.

51. Kathleen Erickson, e-mail interview by author, March 2004.

52. Barkin, interview.

53. Waters, interview.

54. Strada, interview.

55. Kooij, interview.

Chapter 4: The Book Designer: Crafting the Book's Appearance

56. John Reinhardt, "Are There Any Questions?" *John Reinhardt Book Design*, 2004. www.bookdesign.com.

57. Edie Weinberg, e-mail interview by author, March 2004.

58. Christian Fuenfhausen, e-mail interviews by author, April and September 2004.

59. Brian McGroarty, e-mail interview by author, September 2004.

60. Dotti Albertine, e-mail interviews by author, August and September 2004.

61. Helen Robinson, e-mail interview by author, April 2004.

62. McGroarty, interview.

63. Albertine, interview.

64. John Reinhardt, e-mail interview by author, March 2004.

65. Reinhardt, interview.

66. Fuenfhausen, interview.

67. Albertine, interview.

68. Albertine, interview.

69. Susan Newman, e-mail interview by author, July 2004.

70. McGroarty, interview.

71. Reinhardt, interview.

72. Fuenfhausen, interview.

73. McGroarty, interview.

74. Reinhardt, interview.

Chapter 5: The Sales Representative: Getting Books to Readers

75. Roger Saginario, e-mail interview by author, September 2004.

76. Publisher's sales representative (name withheld by mutual agreement), e-mail interview, July 2004.

77. Jonathan David Morris, e-mail interviews by author, August and September 2004.

78. Celeste Risko, e-mail interview by author, September 2004.

79. Bill Wolfsthal, e-mail interview by author, September 2004.

80. Ron Davis, e-mail interview by author, September 2004.

81. Joseph Billingsley, phone interview by author, May 2004.

82. Risko, interview.

83. John Muse, e-mail interview by author, September 2004.

84. Muse, interview.

85. Morris, interview.

86. Muse, interview.

87. Lissa Warren, e-mail interview by author, April 2004.

88. Morris, interview.

89. Muse, interview.

90. Publisher's sales representative, interview.

91. Risko, interview.

92. Katura Hudson, e-mail interview by author, August 2004.

93. Rebecca Fitting, e-mail interview by author, September 2004.

Organizations to Contact

American Booksellers Association
828 S. Broadway, Tarrytown, NY 10591
(800) 637-0037; (914) 591-2665
fax: (914) 591-2720
Web site: www.bookweb.org

This is a nonprofit association of independently owned bookstores.
Its Web site contains research and statistics about book sales.

Association of American Publishers
71 Fifth Ave., 2nd Fl., New York, NY 10003
(212) 255-0200
fax: (212) 255-7007
Web site: www.publishers.org

This is the principal trade association for the book publishing
industry. Its Web site provides industry statistics, articles, and other
information.

The Association of Authors' Representatives, Inc.
PO Box 237201, Ansonia Station, New York, NY 10003
e-mail: info@aar-online.org
Web site: www.aar-online.org

This nonprofit organization keeps literary agents up-to-date about
the field of publishing. All members agree to abide by a Canon of
Ethics. Its Web site includes frequently asked questions.

The Authors Guild
31 E. Twenty-eighth St., 10th Fl., New York, NY 10016-7923
(212) 563-5904
fax: (212) 564-5363
e-mail: staff@authorsguild.org
Web site: www.authorsguild.org

The guild is a professional association for published writers. Its
Web site contains free content for nonmembers, including contract advice and publishing news.

The Children's Book Council
12 W. Thirty-seventh St., 2nd Fl., New York, NY 10018-7480
(212) 966-1990
fax: (212) 966-2073
Web site: www.cbcbooks.org

This trade association for U.S. children's publishers is also the official sponsor of Young People's Poetry Week and Children's Book Week. Its Web site includes information about children's publishers and their submission policies.

Cooper-Hewitt, National Design Museum
2 E. Ninety-first St., New York, NY 10128
(212) 849-8380
e-mail: edu@si.edu
Web site: http://ndm.si.edu/education/index.html

The museum's Web site offers design games and other information of interest to aspiring designers. For New York City students the museum offers programs to learn more about design. For high school students in the area there is a series of free design education programs to introduce them to collegiate opportunities and careers in design.

Editorial Freelancers Association
71 W. Twenty-third St., Suite 1910, New York, NY 10010
(866) 929-5400; (212) 929-5400
fax: (866) 929-5439; (212) 929-5439
e-mail: info@the-efa.org
Web site: www.the-efa.org

Members of this national nonprofit association include self-employed editors, writers, and professionals in related publishing and communications industries.

The National Association of Independent Publishers' Representatives
PMB 157, 111 E. Fourteenth St., Zeckendorf Towers, New York, NY 10003
(888) 624-7779
fax: (800) 416-2586

e-mail: naiprtwo@aol.com
Web site: www.naipr.org

A trade association for book publishers' commissioned reps.

National Coalition Against Censorship
275 Seventh Ave., New York, NY 10001
(212) 807-6222
fax: (212) 807-6245
e-mail: ncac@ncac.org
Web site: www.ncac.org

An excellent reference for learning about current censorship issues.

Society of Children's Book Writers and Illustrators
8271 Beverly Blvd., Los Angeles, CA 90048
323-782-1010
fax: 323-782-1892
e-mail: scbwi@scbwi.org
Web site: www.scbwi.org

This international organization for writers and illustrators of children's books provides conferences, newsletters, and other support for children's writers and illustrators. Its Web site includes an extensive list of college, university, and community-offered courses about writing and illustrating for children.

For Further Reading

Books

Tracey E. Dils, *Young Author's Guide to Publishers*. Westerville, OH: Raspberry Publications, 1996. Contains information on writing, revising, and submitting. Includes book publishers, magazine publishers, and contests for young writers.

Kathy Henderson, *The Young Writer's Guide to Getting Published*. Cincinnati: Writer's Digest, 2001. Explores the publishing process, including practical information such as how to format a manuscript. Features profiles of editors and published young writers. Contains over one hundred market and contest opportunities.

The New Moon Books Girls Editorial Board, *New Moon: Writing*. New York: Crown, 2000. Includes fun writing-related activities and profiles of authors and editors. Also lists publications that accept submissions from young writers.

Joe Rhatigan, *In Print! 40 Cool Publishing Projects for Kids*. New York: Lark, 2003. Includes ideas and instructions for innovative self-publishing projects. Also contains information on the writing process, getting published, and kid-friendly markets.

William Strunk Jr., E. B. White, and Roger Angell, *The Elements of Style*, 4th ed. Boston: Allyn & Bacon, 2000. Excellent reference book on grammar and writing style.

Periodicals

Elizabeth Demers, "Getting a Real Job in Publishing," *Chronicle of Higher Education*, vol. 50, no. 32, April 16, 2004.

Internet Sources

Kelly Milner Halls, "Should These Books Be Banned?" *Denver Post*, September 26, 2004. www.denverpost.com.

Nancy Hanger, "Why Copy Editors Are Necessary: A Small Treatise on the Publishing World," *Windhaven.com*, 2004. www.windhaven.com/copyedit.htm.

Marie Morreale, "Meet the Editor: Arthur Levine," *Scholastic News*, 2004. http://teacher.scholastic.com/scholasticnews.

Carolyn Smith, "A Celebration of Freelancing, Part I: The Freelance Life," *Editorial Freelancers Association*, 2004. www.the-efa.org/celebrationl.html.

Web Sites

American Institute of Graphic Arts (www.aiga.org). This Web site has an excellent resource section for students. It includes an online article, "What in the World Is Graphic Design?" a list of colleges with design programs, and recommended books. It also contains a video about design, an archive of newsletters for students, and a quick quiz on design aptitude.

American Library Association (www.ala.org). Excellent question and answer section about intellectual freedom and censorship. This site also includes fun facts, like a list of the top ten most reread books.

Bookjobs.com (www.bookjobs.com). This Web site was created by the Association of American Publishers to help provide information to students who are interested in working in publishing. It contains a wealth of information, including company profiles, links to publishing study programs, a guide to which majors may fit best with which publishing departments, and a glossary of publishing terms. Free registration provides additional access to job and internship information.

ByLine Magazine (www.bylinemag.com). Monthly print magazine for writers. Each print issue contains student contests. Other contests are available online, along with writers' resources information.

Creative Kids (www.prufrock.com/prufrock_jm_createkids.cfm). A quarterly print magazine created by and for kids. It accepts submissions of cartoons, songs, short stories, puzzles, photographs, artwork, games, activities, editorials, poetry, and plays from eight- to fourteen-year-olds. See the Web site for detailed guidelines and a sample article.

Robin Friedman (www.robinfriedman.com). Friedman is the author of *How I Survived My Summer Vacation: And Lived to Write the Story* and the picture book *The Silent Witness*. Her Web site includes a "For Writers" section, as well as numerous interviews with editors.

Christian Fuenfhausen (www.fuenfhausen.com). This designer's Web site includes sample book covers, interiors, and some redesign work for existing books. Excellent visual examples of what an art director/designer creates.

Kelly Milner Halls (www.kellymilnerhalls.com). Halls has written several books, including *Dinosaur Mummies: Beyond Bare-Bone Fossils, Albino Animals,* and *Dino-Trekking.* Her Web site features an extensive section on "Young Writer Resources."

Kate Harper Designs (http://hometown.aol.com/kateharp/my homepage/business.html). This Web site contains information about a kids' greeting card contest held three times a year to select new quotes for their greeting card line. Writers must be twelve years old or younger. Site includes contest rules, some past winners, and ideas for generating new quotes.

Ellen Jackson (www.west.net/~ellenj). Jackson is the author of more than twenty fiction and nonfiction books for children, including *Turn of the Century* and *Looking for Life in the Universe.* Her site includes the article "Ten Steps to Getting Published."

Johns Hopkins University's Center for Talented Youth (www.jhu. edu/~gifted/imagine/linkB.htm). Contains numerous links to academic competitions, including some in writing and in the arts.

Kid Magazine Writers (www.kidmagwriters.com). Web site for children's magazine writers. Includes a "Kids Write" section that features markets and other information for young writers.

Kids Online Magazine (www.kidsonlinemagazine.com). Founded by a mother and daughter as a place for kids to get published online. The Web site accepts original stories, articles, recipes, craft ideas, poetry, art, and music from anyone up to eighteen years old. They publish all submissions.

Publishing Trends (www.publishingtrends.com). This Web site features articles about book publishing. Archives of past articles are also available.

The Society of Illustrators (www.societyillustrators.org). This Web site contains a research database as well as a career guidance section, which includes a list of art schools that offer courses in graphic design and illustration.

Stone Soup (www.stonesoup.com). This magazine is published every two months and has been in print for the last thirty years. Stories, poems, book reviews, and illustrations are contributed by writers and artists under the age of thirteen. Guidelines as well as highlights from past issues are available online.

Teen Voices (www.teenvoices.com). Quarterly magazine "written by, for and about teenage and young adult women." Accepts submissions from writers and artists under eighteen. A list of suggested topics is available online.

2:25 P.M. (www.marketsforwriters.com/225pm/contents.html). Includes detailed information for student writers, including how to jumpstart the writing process and where to submit for publication.

Word Dance Magazine (www.worddance.com). A quarterly publication designed for and by kids in kindergarten through eighth grade. They publish letters, haiku (a Japanese form of three-lined poems), essays, and stories. Submission instructions and tips are available online.

Writer Beware (www.sfwa.org/beware). This Web site, provided by the Science Fiction and Fantasy Writers of America, contains valuable information for writers of all genres about avoiding common writing scams.

Writer's Digest (http://writersdigest.com). *Writer's Digest* holds monthly contests for kids under thirteen. There are no fees for these short contest entries. Prizes include gift certificates and books about writing. More details are available at the Web site.

WritersMarket.com (www.writersmarket.com). This site for writers includes many resources that are available without a subscription. For example, it offers an online encyclopedia that can be used to research writing-related terms.

Writing-World.com (www.writing-world.com). Features a searchable contest database. Contests for young writers can be found by searching on the category "Youth" in the "Contests" section. An article about checking the legitimacy of contests is included at www.writing-world.com/rights/contests.shtml.

Young Playwrights, Inc. (www.youngplaywrights.org). YPI runs two playwriting contests for writers eighteen years old or younger. One is a national contest and the other is for New York City students.

Young Writer: The Magazine for Children with Something to Say (www.mystworld.com/youngwriter). Published three times a year, featuring writing from children aged five to eighteen, this magazine is based in Great Britain. Writers can submit their fiction, nonfiction, poetry, and opinions by e-mail.

Works Consulted

Books

John F. Baker, *Literary Agents: A Writer's Introduction*. New York: Macmillan, 1999. A series of agent interviews providing information about their role and what it is like to work as an agent.

Judy Blume, ed., *Places I Never Meant to Be: Original Stories by Censored Writers*. New York: Simon & Schuster, 1999. A collection of short stories by young adult writers who have been censorship targets. Includes an introduction by Judy Blume.

Anne Bowling, ed., *2004 Novel and Short Story Writer's Market*. Cincinnati: Writer's Digest, 2003. Market guide for getting fiction published. Contains submission information for magazines, book publishers, contests, and agents.

Marjorie Eberts and Margaret Gisler, *Careers for Bookworms and Other Literary Types*. 3rd ed. New York: McGraw-Hill, 2003. Provides information about career possibilities for bookworms, including careers in book publishing, libraries, research, education, magazines, and newspapers.

Sherry Garland, *Writing for Young Adults*. Cincinnati: Writer's Digest, 1998. An in-depth look at writing for this genre. Also includes chapters on the craft and business of writing.

Information Today, *Literary Market Place 2004: The Directory of the American Book Publishing Industry*. Medford, NJ: Information Today, 2003. Massive directory with more than 14,500 listings. Includes contact information for publishers, agents, and distributors, as well as associations and industry events.

Stephen King, *On Writing: A Memoir of the Craft*. New York: Pocket Books, 2002. Part personal history and part writing advice. Includes anecdotes and examples from his own work.

Bradley J. Morgan, ed., *Book Publishing Career Directory*. Detroit: Gale Research, 1993. The "Advice from the Pro's" section provides an informative series of essays about working in different segments of the publishing industry.

Judith Morgan and Neil Morgan, *Dr. Seuss and Mr. Geisel: A Biography*. Cambridge, MA: Da Capo, 1996. An authorized biography of Dr. Seuss (Ted Geisel).

Andrew Morkes, ed., *Encyclopedia of Careers and Vocational Guidance*. Vols. 1–3. Chicago: Ferguson, 2003. Three-volume set covers nine hundred careers. For each job it includes history, what the job entails, training and education requirements plus ideas for further exploration.

William S. Pattis and Robert A. Carter, *Opportunities in Publishing Careers*. Revised by Blythe Camenson. Chicago: Contemporary, 2001. Includes a discussion of the book industry, preparing for a book publishing career, and what various jobs entail.

Alice Pope, ed., *2004 Children's Writer's and Illustrator's Market*. Cincinnati: Writer's Digest, 2003. Market guide for writing and illustrating for children. Includes essays about children's publishing, insider reports with people in the field, and submission information for hundreds of markets. Contains a special section on markets that publish young writers and artists.

William H. Scherman, *How to Get the Right Job in Publishing*. Chicago: Contemporary, 1983. Although some information is outdated, overall this book provides solid information about various publishing positions. Excellent chapter on the publishing process, "A Year in the Life of a Book."

Thomson Peterson's, *Four-Year Colleges 2005*. Arlington, VA: Thomson Peterson's, 2004. A useful guide for learning about which colleges offer various majors.

Periodicals

Jason Britton, "A New Day for Design," *Publishers Weekly*, October 28, 2002.

Jennifer Ferranti, "Grisham's Law," *Saturday Evening Post*, March/April 1997.

Patricia Fry, "Resources for Young Writers," *Writer's Digest*, April 2004.

Nancy Gibbs, "J.K. Rowling: Reading's Gentle Pied Piper," *Time*, April 26, 2004.

Jim Milliot, "Bowker: Titles Up 19% in 2003," *Publishers Weekly*, May 31, 2004.

———, "Salary Survey," *Publishers Weekly*, July 5, 2004.

Bob Minzesheimer, "10 Years of Best Sellers: How the Landscape Has Changed," *USA Today*, March 11, 2004.

Mary Smith, "What Is Success?" *Idaho Writers League Coeur d'Alene Chapter News and Views*, April 2002.

Brianna Yamashita, "Grooming the Next Generation," *Publishers Weekly*, March 15, 2004.

Internet Sources

American Institute of Graphic Arts, "AIGA/Aquent Survey of Design Salaries 2004," 2004. www.designsalaries.org.

American Library Association, "The Most Frequently Challenged Authors of 2003," 2004. www.ala.org.

Association of American Publishers, "Concluding 2003 on an Upswing: Publishers Recover from Early Year Losses," February 2, 2004. www.publishers.org.

————, "Consumer Books Sales Up Six Percent in 2003," June 4, 2004. www.publishers.org.

The Association of Authors' Representatives, "Frequently Asked Questions," 2004. www.aar-online.org.

Susan Basalla, "The Realities of Jobs in Publishing," *Chronicle of Higher Education*, June 11, 2004. http://chronicle.com.

Bay Area Editors' Forum, "Editorial Services Guide," 2004. www. editorsforum.org.

BBC News, "JK Rowling 'Richer than Queen,'" April 27, 2003. http://news.bbc.co.uk.

Bookselling This Week, "BISG's *Trends* Predicts $44 Billion Book Market in 2008," May 19, 2004. http:/news.bookweb.org.

Bureau of Labor Statistics, U.S. Department of Labor, "Publishing, Except Software," *Career Guide to Industries, 2004–05 Edition*, 2004. www.bls.gov.

————, "Writers and Editors," *Occupational Outlook Handbook*, 2004. www.bls.gov.

Columbia University, "FAQ," Columbia University School of the Arts, Writing, 2004. http://63.151.45.66/index.cfm?fuseaction= WRITING.viewFaq.

CXOnline, "Book Editor," 2004. http://cxonline.bridges.com.

———, "Novelist," 2004. http://cxonline.bridges.com.

Editorial Freelancers Association, "Some Common Rates for Editorial Services," 2004. www.the-efa.org.

Emerson College, Division of Continuing Education, "Information Guide for Certificate in Publishing," 2004. www.emerson.edu.

Robin Friedman, "Steve Meltzer, Managing Editor, Dutton Children's Books," *RobinFriedman.com*, 2004. www.robinfriedman.com.

Graham School of General Studies, University of Chicago, "Economics of Small Press Publishing Certificate Program," 2004. http://grahamschool.uchicago.edu.

Nancy Hanger, "FAQ on Editing/Publishing," *Windhaven.com*, 2004. www.windhaven.com.

Robin Michal Koontz, "10 FAQs About Children's Book Publishing," Society of Children's Book Writers & Illustrators Web site, 2004. www.scbwi.org.

Oberlin College, "Course Offerings," Creative Writing Program at Oberlin, 2004. www.oberlin.edu.

Barbara J. Odanaka, "An Interview with Wendy Lamb," *Skateboardmom.com*, 2004. http://skateboardmom.homestead.com.

Anna Olswanger, "Editor as Writer: A Conversation with Editorial Director Arthur A. Levine," *Writing, Illustrating, and Publishing Children's Books: The Purple Crayon*, 2004. www.underdown.org.

Kathy Paparchontis, "Developmental Editing," Bay Area Editor's Forum Web site, February 24, 1999. www.editorsforum.org.

Publishing Trends, "Changing Channels," May 2003. www.publishingtrends.com.

———, "Dial-a-Rep," May 2002. www.publishingtrends.com.

———, "Dilettante's Dilemma," October 2002. www.publishingtrends.com.

———, "Literary Agents Take Wing," February 2002. www.publishingtrends.com.

John Reinhardt, "Are There Any Questions?" *John Reinhardt Book Design*, 2004. www.bookdesign.com.

Rhode Island School of Design, "Department of Graphic Design Fact Sheet," 2004. www.risd.edu.

Victoria Strauss, "Writer Beware," *Victoria Strauss's Articles*, 2004. www.sff.net/people/victoriastrauss/articles.html.

Patti Thorn, "Celeb Authors Kidding, Right?" *Rocky Mountain News*, October 19, 2002. www.rockymountainnews.com.

Sarah Tomlinson, "Job Q&A: Betsy Lerner," *Monster.com*, 2004. http://sales.monster.com.

Lynn Wasnak, "How Much Should I Charge?" *WritersMarket.com*, 2004. www.writersmarket.com.

Julie Watson and Tomas Kellner, "J.K. Rowling and the Billion-Dollar Empire," *Forbes*, February 24, 2004. www.forbes.com.

Katie Weeks, "Working for Peanuts," *How*, 2004. www.HowDesign.com.

Interviews

Janell Walden Agyeman, e-mail interview by author, September 2004.

Erika Bradfield, e-mail interview by author, April 2004.

Michael Congdon, e-mail interview by author, August 2004.

Anne Garinger, e-mail interview by author, July 2004.

Arthur Levine, e-mail interview by author, September 2004.

Kristi McGee, e-mail interview by author, September 2004.

Josh Mettee, e-mail interviews by author, August and September 2004.

Linda Ramsdell, e-mail interview by author, August 2004.

Lina Shiffman, e-mail interview by author, March 2004.

Anthony Tedesco, e-mail interview by author, July 2004.

Index

Picture Credits

Cover Image: Jeff Paris/Brian Staples
© ANNEBICQUE BERNARD/CORBIS SYGMA, 60
AP/Wide World Photos, 9, 13, 32, 66, 88
© Bryn Colton/Assignments Photographers/CORBIS, 17
© Didier Robcis/CORBIS, 78
Getty Images, Inc., 12
© Jacques M. Chenet/CORBIS, 39
© James Leynse/CORBIS, 21
© Lee Snider/Photo Images/CORBIS, 57
© LWA-Dann Tardif/CORBIS, 15
© Lynsey Addario/CORBIS, 75
© Marc Asnin/CORBIS SABA, 25
Michael Maass, 43, 45, 47, 49, 52, 61, 63
© Reuters/CORBIS, 22, 29, 85
© Richard Berenholtz/CORBIS, 36
© Richard Hamilton Smith/CORBIS, 70
© Robert Llewellyn/CORBIS, 55
© Roger Ressmeyer/CORBIS, 30
© Royalty-Free/CORBIS, 81

About the Author

Yvonne Ventresca has written a number of career-related articles and contributed to a variety of online publications. As a writer, she particularly enjoyed researching and describing the careers for this book. She is grateful to all of the people in the book publishing industry who provided insight into their careers for this guide. Ms. Ventresca has an undergraduate degree in both English and Computer Science, and an MBA in Management. She is currently working on a middle grade novel.